Takini

Amazing Indian Children series:

Naya Nuki: Shoshoni Girl Who Ran
Om-kas-toe: Blackfeet Twin Captures an Elkdog
Soun Tetoken: Nez Perce Boy Tames a Stallion
Kunu: Winnebago Boy Escapes
Pathki Nana: Kootenai Girl Solves a Mystery
Moho Wat: Sheepeater Boy Attempts a Rescue
Amee-nah: Zuni Boy Runs the Race of His Life
Doe Sia: Bannock Girl and the Handcart Pioneers
Takini: Lakota Boy Alerts Sitting Bull

———————

The Truth about Sacajawea, is an accurate paraphrase of the Lewis and Clark journal accounts of the remarkable Shoshoni teenager who spent twenty-one months with the Corps of Discovery. The United States Mint used this book when it developed the new Sacajawea Golden Dollar coin.

Takini

Lakota Boy Alerts Sitting Bull

Kenneth Thomasma

Agnes Vincen Talbot
Illustrator

Grandview Publishing Company
Box 2863, Jackson, WY 83001

**Special thanks
to:**

Fourth and fifth graders at Kelly School
for being good listeners and for naming each chapter

Sioux Indian People
in Eagle Butte and Pine Ridge, South Dakota

Melissa Thomasma
my granddaughter
for all her help and advice

Betty De Vries
for professional help, loyalty, and friendship

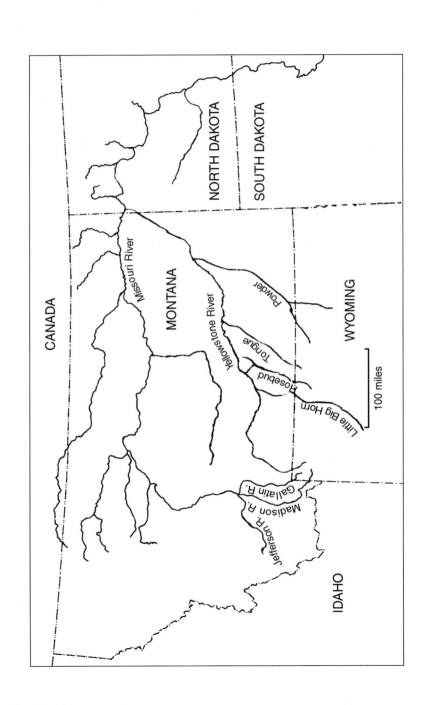

Contents

Preface

Sunday afternoon, June 25, 1876, was the day the final curtain began coming down on a free-roaming people. The Battle of the Little Big Horn and the stunning defeat of George Armstrong Custer and his Seventh Cavalry was a great win for the Indian warriors but they soon would lose the war against their oppressors.

Takini is historical fiction, taking place in the years just prior to the great battle. The story ends at noon the day of the Little Big Horn conflict. Learn through this young Lakota boy's experiences what it was like to be a child trying to understand all the fear and terror felt by women, children, and the elderly.

In an unusual agreement, thousands of Indian people from many bands decided to follow one spiritual leader, Sitting Bull, who was of the Unkpapa Band. The people agreed to follow Sitting Bull's plan of never starting a fight with the bluecoats but at the same time being ready at a moment's notice to defend their women, children, and elders.

Day after day, Takini listens to the words of the great chief. He learns that some of his own Lakota people have already given up and gone to live in the "square teepees" of the white people at a United States Government Agency. Takini hears Sitting Bull say that those who follow him will never give up their freedom and never take handouts from the whites.

Takini is a fictional character living at this significant time in Indian history. He represents all the Indian children who lived through these momentous events and felt their lives change.

1
Survivor

"Screech . . .Scree—ee-ech!!!"

A circling hawk broke the early morning stillness that surrounded a seven-year-old Lakota Indian boy who knelt by a narrow creek, drinking the cool water. The boy raised his head from the water. With sad, bloodshot eyes he stared at the winged form circling his head.

Takini

"O flying friend, can you help me?" the young boy sobbed. "I need help. Please find someone to help me."

Something was terribly wrong. This was a pitiful plea from a pathetic child. He was soaked to the skin from the rain pouring out of dense, low clouds. A strange feeling of quiet sadness filled the damp air.

As the hawk disappeared, the boy bent over the creek once more. This time he filled a hide bag with the cool water. Then he stood and walked slowly away from the creek. Holding the water bag firmly, he began to climb up a small hill.

At the top of the hill, the boy stopped to stare down at a lone teepee. There was no sign of life anywhere. Suddenly, he looked up. There it was, the same hawk, and now it was circling lower and around and around. Then the majestic bird fluttered one of its wings, almost like the hawk was waving at him. The boy had never seen a hawk fly in such a weird way.

"O flying friend, what are you doing? Are you sending me a message? Are you here to help me? Please, please send someone to help me!"

As soon as the boy said this, the hawk banked and flew up through the thick clouds. As fast as it appeared, the

12

Can this circling hawk help this lonely boy?

great hawk was gone. The boy's shoulders slumped as he trudged downhill toward his teepee. The whole area was deserted. There were signs everywhere that at one time many teepees stood in this large campsite. Where had the other people gone? Why was this single teepee still here? Why was there only one small boy in this lonely place? Yes, something was horribly wrong.

With his free hand, the boy pulled back the flap of hide covering the door to his teepee. Inside it was hard to see. His eyes needed time to adjust to the dim light. He moved slowly toward a form lying beneath a buffalo robe. Three other forms lay nearby.

"Mother, I'm back. I have cool water. It will help you feel better."

The woman opened her eyes and managed a smile. Her body was burning with a raging fever. Her face was full of open sores. Her throat was red and raw with pain. She struggled to whisper.

"You are a good son."

With tears streaming down his cheeks, the boy dropped to his knees. He put the waterbag to his mother's lips. As the cool water flowed into the mother's mouth, she began coughing. Water spurted from her lips.

"Thank you, son. I love you so much. Wakan Tanka is calling to me to come to the Spirit Land. The Great Mystery will let my son live. I know you will grow up and be a good and brave man. You will be a servant of our people as your father was. Always remember your father and mother and your sisters. Wakan Tanka will be with you and direct your feet. Talk often with the Great Mystery. He will guide you. The water is good. Thank you for being a loving son. Now it is time for me to sleep."

With those final words, the soft voice of a loving mother fell silent.

This was in 1872 near the Rosebud River in southern Montana. Smallpox had brought death to many, many Indians. In this family it had killed two sisters, a father, and a mother. All four lay silently in their beds near the small boy kneeling next to his mother. At the instant of his mother's death, a strange feeling of warmth filled the boy's body. His tear-filled eyes were suddenly blinded by bright light. The clouds had parted to let the bright sun break through. The teepee was instantly filled with light. With the words of his mother filling his heart, the memory of the hawk flying overhead, and now the sudden sunlight, the boy wondered what all these things meant. *Why did he suddenly feel warm and his body tingle all over?* Something amazing was about to happen. The boy's life was about to change.

Several ridges east of this sad scene, Lakota hunters from the Unkpapa band were desperately searching for buffalo, elk, deer, or any other game animal. Their people were starving and were depending on these hunters to find meat. Most of the millions of buffalo had been slaughtered and left to rot by non-Indians. That was done to make the Indian people helpless. Buffalo had always been the animal Indian people relied on for meat. Hides from these huge animals were used for beds and teepees, bones for tools, and hooves were melted down for glue. The United States Army knew that without the buffalo, Indian tribes would have to give up their freedom and their way of life. The army was ready to do anything necessary to defeat all Indian people and take over their lands. Killing the buffalo would be the key to the army's victory.

In the drizzling rain, the six hunters stopped on a ridge to talk while they ate a meager breakfast. Their voices were gloomy. They wondered aloud if they would ever find any buffalo on this hunt. Should they go toward the rising sun? Should they ride toward the land of the cold winds?

Would Wakan Tanka lead them to buffalo soon? All they could do was pray for success. Their children were hungry. These were men who would never give up and go crawling to a United States Government Agency to beg for food for their families. They decided it would be better to die than to turn into beggars.

As the hunters stood in the drizzle ready to mount their horses and resume the hunt, suddenly the clouds parted and blinding sunlight filled the ridge top. In the west a brilliant rainbow appeared. The men were struck by its instant beauty. Never had they seen a brighter rainbow. The colors were spectacular. Each man knew this had to be a sign from the Great Mystery. They were sure their creator, Wakan Tanka, was sending them a message.

"Oh, my brothers, this is good!" declared one man. "Let us go toward this great beauty coloring the sky. We shall certainly find animals soon!"

Without another word, the excited hunters mounted their faithful horses and rode west toward the rainbow. The men were sure this instant beauty could not be an accident. Its message was clear. Each man was convinced his prayers were about to be answered. This glorious sign would lead them to a successful hunt.

Takini

The six hunters rode side-by-side over a low ridge expecting to see buffalo at any moment. On top of the low rise, without warning one hunter came to a sudden stop. The man raised his hand and began pointing at something.

"Stop!" he shouted. "Look!"

The six riders came to a halt on the hilltop. The man was pointing at a lone teepee where there was no sign of life. The men wondered why there was not a single person or horse in sight. The men could tell it was a Lakota teepee, common to their people. Why was it there? Why had it been abandoned?

One man said, "This is not good. Something is wrong. There is trouble in this valley."

The men quickly rode down the slope to the small stream, through the water, and up the small hill toward the teepee. Twenty feet from the lodge, they reined their horses to a stop. One man slid off his mount and slowly approached the teepee. He pulled the flap open and peered into the room. His eyes met the eyes of the seven-year-old boy. The man noticed the still forms lying about the teepee. Right away the man knew what was wrong. The Death Spirit had come to this teepee. A mother, father, and two small girls lay dead. For some reason only a small boy had survived the visit of the Death Spirit.

"Hurry, my son! Come to me! We must leave this place! Your family is no longer here! Their spirits have left to live with Wakan Tanka! You have been allowed to live! Come, my son! We will care for you!"

As the man spoke, the boy looked at the friendly man who said these wonderful words. When the man finished speaking, the small boy gazed about the teepee. His eyes stopped on each form lying so silently on its bed. When he looked at his mother, he remembered her final words.

"My son, you will be a good and brave man. Wakan Tanka will guide your feet. You will serve your people well as your father did."

Silently the boy promised to honor the mother and father he loved so much. He turned and slowly moved toward the teepee door. He followed the man out. Outside the boy stopped, turned around, put his head into the teepee and spoke softly.

"My family, I love you. I thank Wakan Tanka for giving you to me to love. I will never forget you."

"Come, my son! We must leave now! The Death Spirit could still be in this place!"

Takini

The man took the boy's hand and led him to his horse. The powerful man lifted the boy onto his horse and mounted the animal himself. With one arm around the boy's waist, the man rode off with his friends. The other riders did not have to ask any questions. This wasn't the first time a family or an entire village had been wiped out by disease. The only surprise was finding this boy alive. For some mysterious reason the child was chosen to live.

The six riders moved on toward the rainbow which had already begun to fade. They crossed four small rises when suddenly the lead man jumped from his horse. At the same time his moccasins hit the ground, the hunter had his bow in his hand. In an instant he let an arrow fly with deadly accuracy. A large jack rabbit lay dead just sixty feet away. The men knew it wasn't much, but still they skinned the animal and began chewing the fresh meat. Maybe the strength they gained from this food would help them continue their hunt. Their luck had to change soon, or they would have to give up and return to their families with nothing.

The six hunters dismounted and sat in a circle enjoying the rabbit meat. They talked softly about all the events of the morning. Unknown to them the young boy had wandered away. He had noticed a hawk soaring over-head in the bright sunlight. As the bird circled, it seemed like one of its wings was waving up and down. A marking on its tail was the same marking he had seen on the first hawk which had flown over him as he knelt by the creek. *Could this be the same hawk he had seen near his teepee? Did it return now to send him another message?* The same warm feeling of great peace and happiness filled the boy as it had done earlier. It was something he could not understand.

When the graceful hawk came to rest on a limb of a huge dead tree, it began screeching loudly. The boy immediately followed the ridge line uphill toward the dead tree. Before the men had the rabbit eaten, the boy reached the tree. The loud screeching of the hawk attracted one man's attention.

"Look! The boy has found a friend," the man laughed.

When the boy raised his hands high above his head, one man said, "Yes, and I think he is sending us a signal. Look at him. He wants us to come!"

"Come? Why would we? To see a hawk? I have seen many hawks. You go. You can have a nice visit with the hawk," laughed a second man.

Takini

Without another word, the man trudged uphill toward the boy. As he came closer, the boy waved his arms and pointed toward the valley below him. The man quickened his pace. What could the boy see? The man came to a sudden stop next to the seven-year-old. He dropped to his knees and pulled the boy down next to him. The man could not believe his eyes. There in the valley below was the most beautiful sight imaginable. Over two hundred buffalo were quietly grazing on the rich grasses unaware they were being watched by a boy and a hunter.

Using hand signs, the man told the boy to stay low and wait. Swiftly the hunter dashed down the ridge to his companions. With more hand signs, he gave his friends the exciting news. The men dropped the rabbit, ran to their horses, and followed their leader up the hill. Crouched down on the hilltop, the highly skilled hunters made their plan of attack. They would stay out of sight as they moved to surround the unsuspecting herd on three sides. At a signal from the leader they would move in swiftly for the kill. First, they would use their rifles. Bow and arrows would serve as backup weapons. They must not fail. Off the men rode to begin one of the most important hunts of their lives.

From where the boy stood, he could witness the whole hunt. It was a wonderful thing to see. Keeping out of sight, the hunters had spread out and made nearly a complete circle around the unsuspecting herd. When they were all in position, the signal was given. The six hunters kicked their horses into full gallop. There was mass confusion among the startled buffalo. Having poor eyesight, the lumbering animals were easy targets. In a matter of minutes it was over and seven buffalo lay dead or severely wounded. Four other crippled animals were pursued and brought down. The total kill was eleven.

After prayers of thanksgiving were said, the work began. All eleven animals needed to be butchered and prepared for transport to the village. One man took the boy, lifted him to his horse, mounted up, and rode to the main village for help. Everyone in this Unkpapa village of thirty lodges heard the good news and shouted for joy. The great Chief Sitting Bull was their spiritual leader.

Soon the people were on their way to the kill site. With almost forty adults working, the animals were quickly cut up. Hides, meat, bones, hooves, and all valuable parts were loaded onto travois. Everyone chewed raw tender meat as they worked. Never did meat taste better. Before darkness came, all the loads were safely in the village. Soon the celebration would begin.

While the meat was being stored safely away, Chief Sitting Bull wanted to hear every detail of this amazing day. He listened as the men described the rainbow, finding the boy with his dead family, killing the rabbit, the boy and the hawk, and finally the buffalo. The wise old Chief thought about everything the men had said. He searched for the meaning of each thing that had happened.

Campfires were built, the meat was roasted, and the dancing began. There was great joy and thanksgiving in this Unkpapa village. Late that night Sitting Bull asked for quiet. He signaled all the people to gather at his fire. He took the boy by the arm and had him sit at his feet. All was quiet as the beloved Chief began to speak.

"Wakan Tanka has sent his Unkpapa people many blessings this day. The Great Mystery created a bright rainbow to lead our hunters to the boy at my feet. Then the Great Mystery used this boy as his messenger. The mighty hawk led the boy to a high ridge and let the boy's eyes behold the buffalo herd. The hawk and the boy were used to lead our men to make many kills for our hungry people. I believe Wakan Tanka has spared this boy's life and has given him powerful medicine."

24

Sitting Bull reached down and took the boy by the arm and had him stand. "Stand by me, my son. You have been blessed with life. Wakan Tanka would not let the Death Spirit take you from us. Wakan Tanka has used you to help our people. Now you will receive a new name to mark this special day in your life. From this time on you will be called, Takini."

In the Lakota tongue, Takini, means *Survivor.* The boy stood silently before the people. He knew his life would never be the same. This would be a day which would always live in his memory. And Takini would prove to be a perfect name for this boy who would have unbelievable things happen to him that only the most spiritual people could ever begin to explain. This day was just the beginning of a life of breathtaking events to come. Takini would survive many brushes with the Death Spirit as he lived to carry out his mother's words: "You will serve our people well as your father did."

2
Spirit on the Ridge

Takini was proud of his new name. He would never forget standing next to the Great Chief, Sitting Bull, in front of the people and receiving his new name. The young boy was sure his mother and father would be proud of him and his new name. Takini remembered his mother's teachings and the teachings of his elders. They taught him all animals were his brothers. Even the wind was created by Wakan Tanka, the Lakota name for God. Takini knew the earth was created to provide his people with everything they would need to live a wonderful life. He knew the Great Mystery lived in everything and everyone.

When Takini saw the hawk, he was sure it was sent by Wakan Tanka to lead him to the ridge where he could see the buffalo herd. He believed the rainbow was created to lead the hunters to his teepee to rescue him from the Death Spirit. It all fit together perfectly to help him and the hunters. Next the hawk came to show him the buffalo herd and there was meat to last for many weeks. There were eleven buffalo robes and valuable bones for tools. With all that happened and with his new name, Takini felt very proud indeed.

The young boy was adopted by Sitting Bull himself. Immediately Takini began learning many new skills. With other boys he practiced shooting small arrows at many kinds of targets. The boys were always thinking up new games to play with bow and arrow. Takini remained quiet and let other boys be the leaders. Takini was a good listener and watched the boys who were the best shots with their bow and arrows. Then he would try to copy their methods. Takini quickly became an excellent shot.

Sitting Bull was the chief of the Unkpapa band of Lakota Indian people. There were many different groups belonging to the great Sioux Nation. There were the Sans Arcs, Lakota, Dakota, Yankton, Teton, Brule, Minniconjous, and other bands of Sioux. Many times Takini heard about the awful changes happening to all Indian people. Millions of buffalo were being slaughtered and left on the prairie to rot. White settlers were coming by the hundreds and claiming Indian lands. Railroads and wagon roads were being built. Large armies of soldiers, called "longknives" or "bluecoats" by Indian people, came to force Indians off their hunting grounds.

Some Indian people had already given up. They were called, "those who live with the enemy" because they lived at United States Government Agencies. The government had them living in square teepees and gave them white man's food. Sitting Bull told his people he would never be "one who lives with the enemy." He told all Unkpapa people their Chief would always be a free man, and they too could be free. Takini learned to love Sitting Bull and sat for hours listening to the Great Chief tell story after story. The boy made up his mind to never be "one who lives with the enemy." Like his great leader, Takini would always be free.

Takini

The young boy's first winter with the Unkpapa passed very quickly. He continued to be proud of his new name. He worked very hard to please the great man who had given him his name. Takini thought often about his family. Everytime he did, the boy remembered his mother's loving words. He often repeated the silent promise to someday "be a good and brave man."

As the days of the melting snow came, the Unkpapa people began moving north to hunt. Winter food supplies were running low. Roots and berries were scarce and hard to find in early spring. This would be Takini's eighth summer of life. He was growing fast and getting stronger and stronger. The boy loved to run. Whenever he had a chance, Takini would set out running through the sagebrush. He always headed for the highest place in the area.

Takini loved to reach the top of a ridge and let his keen eyes search every inch of the vast valleys and ridges. This desire to explore the earth would never leave this special boy. It would also lead to unbelievable experiences for Takini, the *Survivor*.

One bright spring day when the trees were turning green, Takini had just left his village and had reached the top of a beautiful ridge. Everything smelled so fresh and alive. A raven soared overhead riding the updrafts of warm air. The boy was deep in thought while he enjoyed the beauty of this spectacular day. He had been standing there for only a few minutes when far below he saw someone walking toward a river which wound through the valley. Takini was too far away to see if this person was a man or a woman.

When the person disappeared into the trees, Takini looked away. He had almost forgotten about this individual when his eyes spotted another movement. At first he didn't know what it was. This moving object was almost hidden by the thick bushes. Suddenly it came into view. Takini saw a bear rise up on its hind legs. He knew instantly it was a Great Bear. Today we call it the grizzly. The huge head and the hump between its shoulders convinced him he was looking at the most powerful animal known to his people. The mighty creature was feared by all who ever came close to one.

Takini was fascinated by the magnificent bear. All Indian people had great respect for the awesome power of the Great Bear. Children were taught to stay far away from this dangerous animal. They were shown the claws from a Great Bear which were as long as a man's fingers and very sharp. Children were told that the Great Bear could outrun any man and with its sharp claws the bear could tear a grown man to pieces in only seconds. The huge animal could weigh four times as much as a large man.

Takini watched the Great Bear drop back to all fours. It began to amble toward the river. Suddenly the boy remembered seeing the person enter the bushes near the same river. Takini realized the man or woman could be right in the path of the slow-moving bear. *Had the bear picked up the human scent? Was it stalking the unsuspecting person?*

Suddenly a hawk came flying into view from the right and began circling the river near the bear. Takini instantly felt the same special feeling he had the last time he had seen the hawk circling above a ridge. The hawk had led him to the ridge to discover the herd of buffalo the hunters were so desperate to find. His mother's words came to him again.

"Wakan Tanka will guide your feet."

With the Great Bear moving toward the unsuspecting person, Takini knew he had to do something fast. He immediately started down the hillside. He tested the wind to make sure his scent would not be carried to the bear and planned his route to be able to keep the Great Bear in view and still stay where he would be hard to see. To lose sight of the bear might cause him to stumble into its path himself.

As Takini moved closer and closer, he suddenly saw the bear stop. With its powerful claws the bear ripped open a log. With its long tongue, the bear began lapping up a swarm of ant larvae. The boy was only fifty yards from the unsuspecting animal. Takini remained hidden in a thick clump of aspen trees. As he watched the Great Bear devour his delicious meal, the boy was startled to see a woman come out of the thick willows next to the river. She carried a tiny baby in a cradleboard on her back. The woman was headed up the hill exactly where the bear was. She could not see the bear and had no idea she was walking toward certain death. In a matter of minutes she would reach the top of the short slope and come within fifty feet of the huge bear.

Takini knew what he must do. Without wasting a second, he walked from his hiding place in the thick aspens and moved straight to the unsuspecting bear. The boy's heart throbbed in his chest. He broke out in a cold sweat. The woman saw Takini and stopped in her tracks. The small boy quickly signaled her to not move and remain quiet. Only ten more steps and the bear picked up Takini's scent. The giant beast rose to a standing position. The huge

The Great Bear charges at Takini.

animal's nostrils flared open, then closed, then flared open again. The Great Bear snorted and let out a deep growl.

Takini spotted the hawk circling above the Great Bear. Calmly he kept walking straight at the fearsome beast. He was ready to give his life to save the woman and her tiny baby. With one final growl, the huge bear dropped to all fours and charged up the hill right at the helpless boy. With the vicious beast only thirty feet from him, Takini quickly raised both hands to the heavens where the hawk still circled.

The boy whispered a prayer to Wakan Tanka, "Please be with me."

Instantly the Great Bear made a sharp right turn and bounded away. Takini could not believe his eyes. The boy dropped to his hands and knees. He was trembling and covered with sweat. He was gasping for every breath. Takini slowly rose to his knees and looked to the sky. The hawk was gone. The boy gave thanks to the Great Mystery for turning the bear away at the last second.

As he stood frozen in place, Takini heard the hawk screeching. *What was the hawk saying? Where was the Great Bear? What made it turn and run north? Was it coming back?* Suddenly the boy felt a tapping on his shoulder. He spun around to face the woman who stood smiling at him.

"You saved our lives. Who are you? Why did you do this brave thing? You have powerful medicine. With your hands held high you turned the Great Bear away and saved me and my baby."

Takini stood without speaking. He quickly looked north to see if the Great Bear was returning. He saw nothing.

"I am Takini. I am of the Unkpapa. Wakan Tanka sent me here. He made the Great Bear leave. We must go before the bear returns. Hurry! I will stay and watch for the bear. You must escape."

As the woman hurried away, she shouted her thanks and blessings to the young boy standing alone on the hillside. When Takini was sure the woman and her baby were safely away, he turned and headed back to his people.

It was several days later when Takini was called by Sitting Bull to come to the chief's lodge. The great Chief was standing near his teepee talking with four strange men. A woman stood off to one side. As Takini approached the men, he recognized the woman in the background. It was the same woman he had saved from the Great Bear. The boy had not bothered telling anyone about how he had stood in front of the bear to protect the mother and her baby. *Why was the woman here now? What were the men saying to Sitting Bull?*

"Takini, my son, come and stand with us, "Sitting Bull ordered. "These men have traveled far. They came to tell me of the great bravery of my son. They told me how you walked into the path of death, offering your life to save a mother and her child. My son, you have done a great thing. The woman you saved is the wife of Chief Spotted Eagle, Chief of the San Arc people. They are our brothers and sisters."

Takini was speechless. He stood, awkwardly, not knowing what to say or do.

Chief Spotted Eagle spoke. "Takini, I have come to thank you. You offered your life to save my wife and newborn son. You have great courage. The Great Mystery has blessed you with powerful medicine. I am thankful. I have brought you a special gift."

Chief Spotted Eagle opened a hide pouch and removed a beautiful necklace. It was made of the claws of a Great Bear. It was the most beautiful necklace Takini had ever seen. The Chief placed it in Takini's hands. The boy examined every detail of the spectacular piece of jewelry. He looked up and managed a smile.

"Thank you, but I do not deserve such a wonderful gift. Wakan Tanka was there with me. He saved me and your wife and child."

Takini

"Takini, I want you to have this necklace. I give it to you because you have given the gift of life to my wife and my son. You will always remain in my memory. I give thanks to the Great Mystery for leading your feet to that hillside that day. You have been given a great gift. I pray your life on this earth will be good and full of happiness. I will never forget you, Takini."

Quickly Takini's story spread through the village. Unkpapa boys and girls begged Takini to show them his bear claw necklace and to tell them his story. Everyone marveled at each detail of the boy's adventure. After telling his story over and over again, finally, Takini slipped away from the village to be alone with his thoughts.

He automatically headed to the top of the nearest ridge and came to the same spot where he had spotted the woman and the bear. Without thinking about it, Takini ambled down to the place where he had stood between the Great Bear and the woman. His curiosity made him walk north in the same direction the bear had run. He crossed a bare hillside and entered a pine forest. There it was, only a few yards into the trees! He was looking down at the reason the bear had left him and the woman and came this way. Between two trees lay what was left of a buffalo calf.

All that remained was part of the skull and some bones. Then Takini was sure that Wakan Tanka had sent the buffalo calf to divert the charging bear, saving the lives of three people. At exactly the right time the Great Bear had picked up the buffalo calf's scent and raced off to a delicious meal.

Standing there next to the buffalo calf's remains, Takini silently gave thanks to the young buffalo for giving its life to save three humans. The boy thanked Wakan Tanka for sending the hawk and for the gift of the buffalo calf. Before Takini lived many more years, the Great Mystery would have more miracles in store for this special boy the Lakota called *Survivor*.

3
Takini's New Friend

A little more than a year later, nine-year-old Takini was in for another wonderful surprise. He was about to receive an amazing gift in a most unusual way. It had been a good winter. There was plenty of food. Many great stories were told around the evening campfires. Some of the stories were frightening. Takini listened to scary talk about soldiers coming to kill Indian people. He heard about how many Indian people were being forced to live in one place in square teepees. The boy wondered why the soldiers wanted to take away the freedom of the Indian people. He didn't understand why the bluecoats wanted to ruin the lives of peaceful Indians.

Takini spent many hours alone thinking about all he had heard. The boy kept Chief Sitting Bull's words in his heart: "We will always be free. We will let no one make us prisoners in our own land. We will never attack any innocent people. We will fight only if we are attacked first. Every brave warrior will fight and die to protect our women and children and elders from the evil ones."

Takini was always looking for the unexpected and for a new adventure. He loved to roam the rolling plains. Today an amazing thing was about to happen, something that would change the boy's life.

The day had begun like most other days. Takini enjoyed a delicious breakfast of buffalo meat roasted over an open fire. Berries, seeds, and wild onions had been ground up and made into tasty cakes. He had done all his work and was free to explore.

Takini was full of energy and ready for a hike to the top of a steep ridge above his village. It was a sunny day and the sky was a brilliant blue. Hunters had already left in search of big game animals. When Takini reached the ridge top, he looked over the valleys and hills that stretched for miles in every direction. It was a peaceful scene of spectacular beauty. Takini thought about all the wonders of the earth. He remembered what he was taught: Mother Earth was created to provide every need he and his people would ever have.

Takini's thoughts were suddenly interrupted by a distant sound. Then an echo rolled through the hills. He thought it sounded like a gunshot. This sound was followed by a loud cry of a wolf or a dog. The boy felt his body tingle. The same powerful feeling was coming over him again. There it was again! The wild hawk was soaring above a narrow place in the valley to the boy's left.

Takini couldn't see the valley floor from where he stood. He had a powerful urge to go down and investigate the sounds. Without another thought, boy ran down the ridge into the first valley. He sprinted up the next hill as fast as he could. His instinct told him he should stay well hidden. Takini was careful to remain in a line of thick bushes. He was convinced there was great danger ahead.

When he came to the top of the next ridge, Takini was glad he could not be seen. He still had a strong feeling that something ahead was dangerous. The hawk continued circling above and was leading him to a spot where he saw a terrifying sight. There, not a quarter of a mile away, bluecoat soldiers on horses were riding two-by-two in a column behind a single rider carrying a brightly colored flag. There were at least sixty soldiers in a long line heading west.

Takini knew he had come close to disaster. He could have been captured or even killed. He did not move or make a single sound but stayed well hidden and was absolutely silent. *Where were the enemy soldiers going? Were they coming to kill Indian people?* Takini knew what he had to do. First, he had to make sure he was not seen, and when the soldiers were well out of sight, he would head back to his village as fast as possible. He had to warn his people before it was too late. A surprise attack could mean the death of many of his family and friends.

While hiding above the bluecoats, Takini suddenly remembered why he had come this way. He was investigating a gunshot and the yelping dog or wolf. Where had these sounds come from? Takini didn't have any idea, but that didn't matter. He knew there was some reason the hawk had led him to this very spot. This time he couldn't stay and wait for an answer. He had no time to waste. He had to get to his people with news of the approaching bluecoats. He was ready to give his own life to stop the soldiers from surprising his people. As soon as the soldiers were out of sight, Takini would start on a desperate run to warn his village.

As Takini watched the last soldier disappear into the distant trees, he turned to run when he saw something moving slowly through the deep grass. It looked like a dog. *Why was it just barely moving? Why did it seem to be dragging itself along?* There was no time to investigate.

Takini turned away and ran at top speed straight for his village. He had to make it back as fast as possible without falling which would waste valuable time. To break a leg in a fall would mean disaster and even death. Takini was gasping for every breath. His heart pounded in his chest. Sweat poured from his body. He was using every ounce of strength he had to get the news to his people.

At the ridge above Takini's village, a Lakota warrior watched the boy come running up the final hill. The man rode his horse directly into Takini's path about fifty feet from the exhausted boy.

"Takini!" the man shouted, "You run like the deer! Why do you hurry?"

Between gasps for breath the boy shouted, "Enemy soldiers are coming!"

Takini

The man reached down and hoisted Takini onto his horse. They raced down hill to the village and straight to Sitting Bull. The great chief listened to his adopted son tell about the column of sixty bluecoats riding west. Instantly Sitting Bull turned to three men standing near him. He ordered the three warriors to leave immediately, find the soldiers, and watch their every move. Next he sent out the order for all people to take down their teepees, pack their belongings, and prepare to move

"Takini, you are a good son. Now you must go with our three scouts. Take them to the place where you saw the bluecoats. You can save them much time. Be brave and serve our people well. May Wakan Tanka be with you," Sitting Bull said.

The boy rode double with one of the scouts. He directed the men to the place where he had stood watching the bluecoats. The man let Takini down.

"You have done well, boy. We will track the bluecoats. You have done your work. Now you can return to the village and escape with our women, children, and old people."

Takini watched the three scouts head into the valley to pick up the trail of the sixty soldiers. Before he turned to leave for his village, he noticed the hawk had returned. Suddenly it all came back to the boy. The gunshot, the yelping sound, and the slow-moving dog caused him to wonder what it all meant. He had to unravel the mystery.

Takini moved downhill very slowly, staying in the tall grass and bushes so he couldn't be seen very easily. When he reached the place he had last seen the slow-moving dog, he was shocked to see blood on the grass. He examined the bloody grass. The blood was quite fresh and left a trail easy to follow. As he passed a clump of bushes, the silence was broken by a piercing howl of great pain. The boy raced toward the sound. Only thirty feet away a vicious attack was underway. A pack of hungry wolves had been attracted to a wounded dog. The first wolf had just pounced on the pitiful animal. Soon the pack of wolves would tear the helpless dog to pieces.

Takini grabbed a rock and picked up a large sturdy stick. With perfect accuracy, the boy let the rock fly. The missile hit the wolf in the ribs with tremendous force. The wolf rolled completely over, screeching in pain. It bounded off into the trees howling loudly. The boy charged toward the remaining wolves swinging his stick in a large circle above his head.

The entire pack of wolves retreated into the trees as Takini approached the injured dog. The boy looked down at the awful sight. The dog had been shot in the neck.

Takini

Blood oozed from the wound. The animal lay on its side, its eyes full of pain and fear. The boy dropped to his knees five feet from the pitiful dog. He inched forward very slowly. The terrified animal managed a weak growl causing Takini to pause. Only an arm's length from the dog, Takini lowered his open hand toward the dog's nose. An open hand would comfort the frightened animal.

"Good dog," whispered Takini. "I will not hurt you."

The dog sniffed the boy's fingers. Then the pathetic animal even licked the boy's fingers. Cautiously Takini rubbed the dog's back and neck. The animal began to whimper and whine. He seemed to know Takini was there to help him. Over his shoulder the boy could see the eyes of two wolves peering at him. Very slowly Takini moved toward some nearby rocks. With deliberate movements the boy grasped a rock in each hand. In a second the boy was on his feet and had fired a rock at the wolves. The second rock was on its way before the first rock landed. When the second rock landed, a shrill howl filled the air. It had found its mark. The wolves would not be returning as long as Takini was there.

Takini knelt next to the wounded dog for a few minutes more. Then he quickly headed to the creek and returned with a hide sack of cool water. He let the dog lap water

Takini guards the wounded dog.

from his hands cupped together. He dripped small amounts of water on the open wound and cleaned it as best he could. After pressing a piece of hide against the wound, the bleeding finally stopped.

The boy thought about what he should do next. The dog was too big to move. It had to weigh almost a hundred pounds. The animal had beautiful markings. Its fur was grayish white. It had a black head and one white ear. Takini had never seen a dog like this one. The animal seemed to understand that the boy was a friend, and the terrified dog had begun to relax. The dog could not be left. The wolves were sure to return to finish the job. Takini decided to stay.

Hours passed, and the day was about to end. The boy was sure his people had moved far away to a new camp. The longer Takini waited, the farther he would have to go to get back to the safety of his village. Strangely, the boy felt perfectly safe. It was almost as if Wakan Tanka was there with him and the helpless dog. He had a deep feeling that he was doing what the great Creator wanted him to do.

Just before dark, Takini gave the injured dog more water. As the boy rubbed the dog's back, the animal lifted its head a few inches from the ground and licked Takini's hand.

"Good dog. You are getting stronger. You will get well. I will stay by your side. Good dog," whispered Takini.

The boy had already pulled lots of long grass, spreading it on the ground to make a mattress. There was plenty of grass for a mattress big enough for him and the injured dog. Takini gathered a good supply of rocks and was ready should the wolves decide to return. Gently the boy moved the dog to the grass mattress. He talked softly as he slid his hands under the animal's head and shoulders. Inch-by-inch Takini moved the dog's head and shoulders onto the mattress. The pitiful animal whined and whimpered but its eyes were full of signs of trust.

With the sun gone, the air cooled and it was getting colder and colder with every passing hour. Takini lay against the large dog so they could share each other's warmth. The boy would be awake most of the long cold night, dozing off for only a few minutes at a time. When light first appeared in the eastern sky, Takini had fallen into a deep sleep. He was dreaming when suddenly he felt a rough tongue licking his face. His eyes opened. There sat the big gray dog, now strong enough to sit up.

"Good morning, dog. I see you are feeling better. I am happy," whispered Takini.

The groggy boy raised his hand and stroked the dog's large head. The dog licked the boy's bare arm as Takini pushed himself to a kneeling position. The boy's eyes blinked. He was stiff and tired. His stomach made strange sounds. He realized he had not eaten for a whole day. He had to do something soon. He couldn't stay at this place much longer. He had to move, but he had no idea where his people might be. Takini stroked the dog's head one more time, then rose to his feet.

Takini picked up his hide bag and began walking toward the creek. He was on his way to get more water for the injured dog. After his bag was filled with clear cool water, the boy turned to return to the dog. As he turned, he saw a wonderful sight. There stood the dog wagging his tail.

"Good dog! You are doing better! Can you follow me? Let's see! Maybe we can leave this place!"

As the boy moved south, he was happy to be on his way again with his new friend at his heels. The dog's recovery was amazing. Takini was careful to not move too fast and to check on the dog often. He stopped many times to give the dog a rest and a drink of water. It did not take long to reach the site of his people's village. Everyone was gone, leaving a trail that would be easy to follow.

Takini was very hungry. He had not eaten in a long time. Suddenly he remembered something about his village. He headed straight to some tall trees on the edge of the village site. The boy looked up and smiled. There high above his head in a large tree, hung two buffalo hindquarters. In their hurry to leave his people had left them hanging there, out of the reach of hungry bears. A few delicious slabs of meat still clung to the large bones.

Takini had to climb only a short way to untie the hide rope holding the hind quarters from a large limb. Then he was able to loosen the rope tied around a smaller branch and then lower the bones and meat to the ground. In no time the boy and the starving dog were enjoying the delicious morsels of buffalo meat. Takini quickly cut strips of meat and stuffed them into his food bag.

"Dog, you liked the meat! Now we go! We must find my people! We will not let the bluecoats find us or surprise our people!"

Off the two friends moved following the trail of Takini's people. The boy hoped his people were safe. He said a prayer to Wakan Tanka to protect those he had come to love as his new family. With all his senses alert for any sign of danger, Takini and the dog moved as fast as possible. He realized the soldiers could be anywhere. Maybe they were watching him at this very moment. The boy had heard the horrible tales of soldiers killing men, women, and even children and old people. He knew bluecoats had burned entire villages while Indian people tried to escape. Takini could not understand such evil. He was sure no Lakota warrior would ever kill helpless women, children, and old people. Only vicious cowards would do such terrible acts of hate. Takini became even more alert and careful. The enemy eyes must not see him.

4
The Unwanted

With the dog following close on his heels, Takini
walked all day. He tried to stay in bushes and trees whenever possible and avoided all open areas where he could be
seen. As the sun dropped below the western hills, Takini
believed they were getting close to his people's new village.
The trail was much fresher now. He had already passed a

place where his people had spent a night on their way to a more permanent camp. The boy was anxious to return to the safety of his village.

Takini knew he could not travel in the darkness. It would be impossible to see any danger. He and the dog could walk right into an enemy camp or walk right into the path of a great bear or mountain lion. The boy was wise enough to know he must stop for the night. He headed for a tangle of bushes and burrowed into the middle of them. In the thicket he cleared a space large enough for him and the dog to lie down. Once more the boy and the dog curled up together for a long night. This night was warmer, and Takini slept much better.

The next morning, the two friends enjoyed some of the leftover meat and some clear cool water.

"Let's go, dog! We're almost home!"

Takini took off at a brisk pace, headed up a small hill, following the trail of the Unkpapa people. Just before they reached the top of the hill, the dog suddenly stopped right in front of the boy. Takini almost fell over the animal.

"What are you doing, dog? I could have fallen on top of you! Is something wrong? What are you trying to tell me?"

Takini dropped to his knees. He was sure there must be trouble nearby. The dog would not act this way for no reason.

"Good dog," whispered Takini. "Let's find the trouble."

With the dog at his side, Takini carefully crawled the rest of the way to the top of the hill. The boy was barely able to see over the hill. When he did get a good look, he was stunned. Not fifty feet away a mountain lion was tearing an elk calf to pieces. Takini was close enough to the dangerous beast to see the big cat's whiskers. Slowly the boy crawled backward out of sight of the great animal. He was glad the wind was blowing toward him and not carrying his scent to the mountain lion.

Takini quickly changed his course and traveled in a large arc around the mountain lion. Finally making it back to his people's trail, the boy trudged on in his attempt to get to his people without delay. The day wore on and the afternoon seemed long. Takini was weary and wondering if he would reach his people. He didn't want to spend another night in the open.

Late that afternoon, Takini walked in a shallow valley near a small stream. After enjoying a cool drink from the creek, the boy looked up at a ridge of rugged rock. There he saw a beautiful sight. A hawk circled above the rocks and came in for a perfect landing. He flapped his wings several times.

Takini

"O great winged hawk, what message do you have for me today? Do you see danger? Do you see my people? O great messenger, what is your message?"

Takini made his way up the ridge, into the rocks, and found an opening which would allow him to look out without being seen. The boy felt like shouting for joy. There, in the meadow below, he saw his people busily erecting their teepees. Takini squeezed between the rocks and began running down the hillside. Six village dogs came charging toward him and the strange dog he had at his side.

Takini thought the village dogs would attack his new friend. The boy shouted at the charging dogs and brandished his stick, warning the dogs to behave. The hair on the back and neck of Takini's new dog was standing straight up. He was as big or bigger than any of the village dogs. Suddenly the pack of dogs calmed down, and the circling and sniffing began. Takini dropped to his knees and gave his new dog a hug. He was sending the village dogs a message that his dog was here to stay.

Sitting Bull's uncle, Four Horns, was the first person to reach Takini. "My son, I am happy to see you. We were afraid the longknives had captured or killed you. You were very brave when you came with news of the enemy. Then

you bravely helped our scouts find the enemy. This saved
our people from having a horrible battle. Takini, we wondered why you did not return."

Takini started to tell his story of saving the dog when
Four Horns stopped him. "You can talk later, my son.
Come!" laughed Four Horns. "Our great Chief wants to
see his son!"

Sitting Bull was resting on a log near his lodge. His two
wives were putting everything in its place. Spruce branches were being covered with buffalo robes to make comfortable beds. A fire already burned brightly. The great
man motioned for Takini to come and sit next to him.

"Takini, my brave son, it is good to have you back. I see
you have found a new friend. The dog already loves you.
Where did you find this dog? I'm sure you have a story to
tell our elders tonight. You have been given many gifts by
the Great Mystery. Wakan Tanka dwells in you, my son.
He has blessed you with powerful medicine. Be sure you
pick a good name for your new friend."

Before the campfire that night, Takini did pick a name
for his new dog. He remembered hearing the story of a
brave warrior. This warrior rode his horse out to meet
many enemy bluecoats alone. The soldiers fired many bul-
lets at the warrior. Dozens of shots whizzed past the war-

rior's head. Not a single bullet touched the daring warrior. His name was Lone Dog. It would be a perfect name for the dog he had saved from death. Takini would call his new dog, Lone Dog.

That night, Takini told his story to eager listeners. The elders laughed when the boy said he named his new dog, Lone Dog. Lone Dog, the warrior, laughed the loudest. Later, the brave warrior told Takini he showed great wisdom when he decided to call his new dog, Lone Dog.

For the next year, Takini and his dog went everywhere together. Before the end of the boy's ninth summer, he would find yet another loyal friend. This time the Unkpapa people would be even more amazed by this boy's special powers.

The Unkpapa people moved from place to place often. They constantly searched for good food for their horses and good places to hunt. Today, as Takini's people were moving to a new location to set up their village, storm clouds began building in the west. Gigantic thunderheads towered thousands of feet into the sky. Thunder rumbled in the nearby mountains. As the thunder became louder and louder, Takini's people knew they needed to find a campsite before the storm hit. With six other boys, Takini herded the extra horses toward the next camp.

High in the mountains, just west of the fast moving people, a cloudburst sent rain pouring down, filling every creek and river. The people had just reached the valley floor and the Powder River. Usually the Powder River was a shallow, slow-moving stream. A person could easily walk all the way across with water only ankle deep in most places. Now it was a fast-moving river already three feet deep and getting deeper and deeper with every passing minute.

Without hesitating the people entered the swiftly moving water. The horses carried their riders safely to the other side. No one had any trouble making the crossing. Four Horns held Takini in front of him on his faithful horse as they forded the river. Lone Dog swam next to the horse. The pouring rain hit as soon as Takini's feet touched the ground. The sudden downpour sent the people scurrying to get under their teepee hides. They grabbed the hides and crawled under them to wait out the storm. Takini pulled Lone Dog under a large hide being held up by Four Horns. Everyone was soaked before they could get under their hides.

The rain came down harder and harder. It rained over two inches in less than thirty minutes. When the downpour finally let up, people began to grab their teepee poles so they could erect their lodges before the next deluge of rain hit. Takini and his friends checked on the horse herd. The animals were all grazing quietly on the lush grasses. Everything seemed back to normal when suddenly Takini heard a loud whinning sound. Next to the roaring river a mare dashed back and forth along the bank.

Takini ran to the river to investigate. He knew this mare. She had a colt which the people said was the worst animal they had ever seen. This mare's colt never let a human being get near it. Just a year before, the unruly colt kicked a teenage boy, causing serious injuries. Now this wild colt was in big trouble. It had not crossed the river with the rest of the animals. There it was, trotting back and forth next to the raging river. The water was now over five feet deep. The powerful current was extremely dangerous.

As Takini reached the riverbank, he saw terror in the bulging eyes of the frantic mare. She was desperately calling to her colt as if she was urging him to swim the river. The boy began to experience that special feeling coming over him again. He knew what he had to do. Lone Dog had needed his help. Now the colt needed him. The boy grabbed a braided hide rope. He ran to the mare and tossed a loop of rope over her neck. Takini had ridden a horse alone only a few times. He had never ridden a horse across a wild river. Now he was ready to try it. The colt would not survive the crossing alone. With the rope securely over the mare's head, Takini leaped onto her back and began urging the large horse into the raging water.

"Stop, Takini! Forget the colt!" Four Horns screamed. "He's no good! He's not worth risking your life to save!"

The man's words were lost in the crashing thunder that followed exploding lightning just east of the river. With one hand, Takini gripped the rope and with the other he held onto the mare's long mane. The powerful horse plunged into the angry river. The boy was instantly drenched in cold, muddy water. Takini coughed and gagged. He was nearly swept from the mare's back and was barely able to hang on against the mighty thrust of water.

The struggling mare moved forward by inches. She was straining to keep her head above the crashing waves. Driven by a mother's love, she fought her way toward her colt. Takini was horrified. He slowly began to lose his grip on the mare's wet mane. He couldn't hold on much longer. Could this be the end for the courageous boy? Suddenly the mare was propelled straight downstream. Takini thought she would never make shore now, but the mare knew what she was doing. The wise horse let the current

Takini rides the frantic mare across
the raging river toward her colt.

carry her on an angle toward the nearby bank where the river took a turn.

Ten feet from safety, Takini lost his grip on the mare's mane. He was instantly swept into the raging water. With the rope twisted around his wrist, the boy disappeared under the angry waves. With all his remaining strength, Takini desperately tried to pull himself up for air. His lungs were bursting. It was no use. No matter how hard he tried, he could not reach the surface. He was sure this was the end. Just as he began to think that Wakan Tanka had abandoned him, the mare's hooves hit the river bottom. She dug in and battled her way to the river's bank. With his lungs about to explode, Takini's head burst above the wild water. He gulped in the most precious air he had ever breathed. What a glorious feeling it was to be able to breathe again!

Digging in her hooves, the determined mare hauled Takini up the bank before he had time to release himself from the hide rope. Quickly he freed himself and ended up sitting on the muddy riverbank gasping for oxygen. The boy rubbed the muddy water from his eyes. As his eyes cleared, Takini looked up. There only twenty feet away the mare was nuzzling and licking her colt. The young horse rubbed against his mother's side. Takini smiled as he finally was able to rise to his feet.

Takini

The boy realized he was once more separated from his people. There was no way he would try crossing the river until it calmed down and the water receded. It would be the next morning before a safe crossing could be attempted. Takini slowly moved toward the mare and her colt. He talked to the mare as he approached her. He made sure he kept the mare between him and the unpredictable colt. Everyone believed the mare's colt was possessed by evil spirits. No one dared go near it. Four Horns owned this ornery colt. Many times he tried to give it away, but no one would have anything to do with it.

As Takini came closer to the mare, the colt came around its mother and looked right at the approaching boy. "Young one, only your mother loves you. Why are you so wild? Why aren't you like other colts? Why do you have to act so crazy?"

The young horse just stood staring at Takini with its ears turned toward the boy as if it could understand every word he said. Takini walked up to the mare, still keeping the mare between him and the colt. The boy softly stroked the big mare's neck.

"Good girl," Takini whispered. "You love your wild colt. You are a good mother."

The mare made soft sounds through her nose and mouth. She rubbed her snout against the boy's shoulder.

Takini had not noticed that the colt started moving around its mother. Without a sound the young horse came up behind the unsuspecting boy. Suddenly the colt pushed his nose between his mother and Takini. The startled boy stepped back. The colt followed him. The boy reached out slowly and stroked the colt's neck. A warm feeling flooded over Takini. He was sure the young horse understood what he had done. *Could the mare have told her colt about Takini? Could horses talk?* Many times Takini would think about these questions. He wondered how long amazing things would keep happening to him.

Once again he thought about his own mother, and how she said Wakan Tanka would be with him throughout his life. There were many amazing adventures ahead for Takini. People would continue to see evidence of this boy's powerful medicine. Even the worst enemies of the Lakota people would be baffled and confused by Takini's powers. The Great Mystery had many surprises in store for the Lakota and this special boy.

5
Another Miracle

That night Takini lay next to the colt as it slept on the ground beside its mother. The mare slept standing up next to her colt. The young horse's body provided some warmth for the boy as he slept off and on. After a long cold night, the colt stood up and the movement awakened

Takini

Takini. He was stiff and sore and shivered in the early morning cold. The boy rubbed his eyes and slowly moved to the riverbank. The Powder River was quiet and shallow again. It was almost back to normal.

Suddenly the silence was broken by the sound of a barking dog. Takini smiled as he watched Lone Dog plunge into the river and paddle toward him. In only a few minutes Lone Dog was climbing the riverbank and racing to Takini. The excited dog jumped up to lick the boy's face.

"Good dog! Good dog!" Takini laughed.

He dropped to his knees and hugged the big dog. Then Takini felt something pushing against his shoulder from behind. The colt's wet nose was rubbing against Takini's arm. Lone Dog began growling at the colt.

"No, Lone Dog! Be still! The colt is all right. Be good to him!" Takini urged.

Lone Dog seemed to understand, and wagged his tail.

"Come on, Lone Dog. Let's go home!"

Once again Takini slipped the braided loop over the big mare's head. Then he took a few quick steps and jumped onto her back. Soon the mare, her colt, and Lone Dog were in the water headed for the other side and the Unkpapa village. Four Horns was standing on the far bank waiting for

Takini. The man could hardly believe his eyes. The boy rode the mare up the bank and over to Four Horns who stared at the colt. The once wild colt now seemed almost normal. Takini dropped to the ground next to the colt.

"Watch it, boy! That colt will kick your insides out!" Four Horns warned.

Pretending that he couldn't hear a word Four Horns had said, Takini moved to the colt's side and softly rubbed the young horse's neck. All the while, Takini continued talking softly to the amazingly calm young horse.

"Takini, what happened to the wild one?" asked the surprised Four Horns. "Did you use your magic and powerful medicine to drive the evil spirits from the crazy one?"

"I think the mare spoke to her colt," answered Takini. "She used her power to change her colt. I think she told her colt to be friendly."

"My boy, you are amazing! Takini, the colt is yours if you want him. You can try to train him. You can be his master. Give the colt a name. He's yours!" Four Horns proclaimed. "What will you name him?"

"I will name him Friendly. That way he will have to learn to live up to his name. He will never do bad things again," Takini predicted.

Takini

He wasted no time and began training Friendly that very day. With Lone Dog at his side Takini spent many hours with the mare and her colt. He walked with them. He took time to stroke and rub the colt's neck and back. After five days and many hours shared with the mare and Friendly, the boy finally approached the colt with a braided rope. Friendly never had a rope around his neck, so this was a very dangerous thing to attempt. Takini spoke soothing words as he stroked Friendly's neck and rubbed his ears. He held the rope up to let the colt sniff it. After fifteen minutes of soft talk and gentle strokes, Takini slowly slipped the loop over Friendly's head. The colt snorted and began pawing the ground with his right front hoof.

"Good boy! Good horse! It's all right, Friendly," Takini whispered in the colt's ear as he stroked the young animal's neck.

In only a few seconds Friendly calmed down completely. Soon Takini was using the rope to lead Friendly on short walks. The colt's mother followed close behind like nothing had changed. With only a few days of practice leading Friendly on longer walks, the boy slowly raised himself onto the colt's back, expecting the young horse to start bucking. Friendly stayed as calm as a horse that had been ridden for years. Four Horns was watching from a distance. The man thought he would never see the day when the wild colt would be ridden. Now he was watching Takini ride the unruly animal on the first try with no problem. Four Horns could hardly believe his eyes. The colt didn't buck, not even once. Off rode Takini with the mare trotting along, and Lone Dog bounding on ahead.

After that day, Takini and Friendly were always together. Each day they traveled farther than the day before. Takini was the happiest boy on earth. He was able to explore many more beautiful places. He never tired of discovering a new valley and a new stream. Wakan Tanka had created a wonderful earth that provided everything the Indian people needed to live a good life. Friendly was skillful and able to gallop across the land while avoiding badger holes and other hazards along the way. Lone Dog was always running back and forth, sniffing everywhere. The three friends were sharing many wonderful adventures.

Takini also spent lots of time listening to the great chief, Sitting Bull. The boy loved to hear the honored man's words and all the wisdom he shared with his Unkpapa people. Takini tried to remember every word the wise man spoke. Sitting Bull loved his people and loved the freedom they enjoyed. The chief continued to worry about the future of his people. Soldiers kept coming to the beautiful land in greater and greater numbers. Wagons and hundreds of Europeans traveled the rough roads. Sitting Bull asked his people to stay away from the "longknives" and the white people. Never were they to start a fight or harm any innocent people. He told the young men to control their anger, but always be ready to fight back if ever attacked.

Sitting Bull loved his own family very much. He was generous and gave all his children many wonderful gifts. He taught his children to be both brave and kind. He urged them to think good thoughts and always be ready to help people who were in need.

Early one beautiful spring morning, Sitting Bull walked to the edge of the village. Takini did not see the great man coming. The boy was feeding Lone Dog some dry meat while Friendly was grazing on the sweet grasses.

"My son, your animals love you. They know you love them," the chief proclaimed.

For a few seconds Takini was startled by the surprise visit by the great man. The boy wondered why the chief had come to visit him and didn't know what this could mean. Takini thought maybe he had done something wrong. It didn't take long for him to learn the reason for the chief's visit.

"Takini, Wakan Tanka is good to you. The Great Mystery has given you many special gifts. Now it is the time in your life to go off to be by yourself. You can find a special place to sit alone and speak with Wakan Tanka. Do not eat or drink. Do not sleep. Spend three days waiting for the Great Mystery to come to you with a special vision for your life which will make you an even better person. Before you leave, prepare yourself for this test. Do not be afraid. Do not give up. Wakan Tanka will be with you."

Takini stood listening to every word the great chief said. He knew what these words meant. All spiritual Lakota people left their village at least once a year to be alone in the wilderness fasting, praying, and asking Wakan Tanka to send them a vision for their future on this earth. Without food, water, or sleep for three days, the body and mind would be purified. It would take great strength and determination to resist the temptation to quit early. Takini was excited to try this life-changing adventure. His body tingled all over with excitement.

Takini was out early the next day, running to find Friendly. Lone Dog bounded away in front of the boy. The dog knew there was a great day ahead. Takini found Friendly grazing just outside the village.

"Friendly, it's a beautiful day! Let's go see the wonderful places the Great Mystery has created for us! Lone Dog! Come! Let's go!" Takini shouted.

With a full food bag tied to his waist, the boy and his animal friends were on their way for a day of adventure. Takini made sure he would have extra to share with Lone Dog. He had packed many pemican cakes and lots of dried meat. The boy had a special reason for this ride. He planned to search for a place to sit and fast and talk to Wakan Tanka as Sitting Bull suggested. Takini had no idea his search would be stopped short. Something was already happening that would interfere with his plan.

For two hours the boy rode Friendly up and down the rolling hills. At the top of one of the hills, Takini signaled Friendly to stop. The view here was spectacular. He could see for miles and miles. Looking over the rolling plains, Takini saw a rocky ridge towering over the surrounding hills. One ledge rose high above the rocky ridge.

"Friendly, can you see that ridge? That's where we'll go! Can you make it? Sure you can! You can go anywhere! You're the best horse in the world! Let's go!"

Before Friendly could get started, Lone Dog barked. Then he suddenly turned and bounded off in the opposite direction. Why was the dog racing away? What had gotten into Lone Dog?

"Lone Dog! Where are you going? Come back! We're going the other way! What's the matter with you?"

Lone Dog ignored Takini's shouts. The dog continued to race down the hillside at full speed. Then the boy saw it. There in the distance a hawk circled around and around, gliding on the rising air currents. Takini felt the powerful feeling come over him as it always did when something surprising was about to happen. Immediately the boy turned Friendly around and began following Lone Dog down the hill. What could the dog know to cause him to suddenly race away?

Friendly could not gallop at top speed. The hillside was too steep and was covered with loose sand and rock. It would be easy to topple over and seriously injure himself and Takini. At the bottom of the hill, the boy looked up at the next ridge. There, at the top, stood Lone Dog his tail wagging wildly.

What's going on? Takini wondered aloud. What is Lone Dog trying to tell me? Maybe I will find out at the top of the ridge! Let's go, Friendly!"

Takini

The boy urged his faithful horse up the ridge. Friendly's ears were turned forward as if the horse was trying to hear something ahead of him. Lone Dog was more excited than ever. He was still barking and now began to spin around in circles. Takini was sure the dog had discovered something unusual to cause him to become so excited. The boy knew there might be danger waiting in the next valley, so near the crest of the ridge. Takini dropped to the ground. Holding Friendly's reins, the boy called Lone Dog to come to his side. He gently grabbed the dog's nose to signal him to be quiet.

"Lone Dog! Stay!" Takini whispered. "Good dog! Be quiet!"

As the boy looked around, he was surprised to see nothing unusual anywhere. All he could see was another peaceful valley. There was no movement anywhere. Takini saw a small creek meandering through the valley floor. Willow bushes, cottonwood trees, and a few spruce trees lined the banks of the small stream.

"Lone Dog, what is it? Why did you lead me way over here? Are you playing a trick on me? There's nothing to see. Are you just thirsty?"

The dog licked Takini's face, kept wagging his tail, turned, and dashed down toward the creek. Suddenly the hawk flew from a cottonwood branch and began gliding on the air above a small clump of spruce trees.

"O one who flies above, have you come with another message? What are you here to tell me? Is there something in the trees below your wings? You are my friend. I will come to see what your message is today. Go, Friendly! We came this far. Let's see what Lone Dog and the flying messenger are trying to tell us."

Before Takini and Friendly reached the creek, Lone Dog had already disappeared into the trees and bushes. At the edge of the bushes and trees, the boy jumped from his horse. He tied Friendly to a small cottonwood tree and made his way into the willows where he had seen Lone Dog disappear from view. Takini moved slowly, stopping often to listen for any sound. All he could hear was the creek spilling over its rocky bottom. Then the stillness was broken by the sound of Lone Dog whimpering. The boy followed the sound which led him to the edge of the creek. Takini was shocked to see Lone Dog standing over the body of a young boy. The dog was licking blood from the boy's forehead.

"Good dog," Takini whispered. "Is he dead? Sit! Let me see!"

Takini helps an injured young boy.

Takini carefully examined the injured boy. He was still breathing. He had a huge bump on his forehead with a cut that sent blood over his face. The boy's legs were hanging over the edge of the creek. It looked like the boy was crossing the creek and fell from his horse, striking his head on a nearby rock. Takini gently slid his arms under the injured boy's shoulders and arms. He carefully pulled him away from the creek. Lone Dog paced back and forth crying softly and waging his tail.

"You are a good dog, Lone Dog. You were sent to find this boy. Wakan Tanka wanted you to show me the way. He wants us to help save this boy's life. Lone Dog, we can do it."

While talking to Lone Dog, Takini emptied his food bag and filled it with water. He took the water to the injured boy and used it to clean the cut on the boy's head. It looked much better with the caked blood washed away. Most of the bleeding had stopped. For an hour Takini worked to make the boy more comfortable. He pulled armfuls of grass to make a pillow for the boy's head. He kept sprinkling cool water on the large bump. The swelling had already gone down a little. Takini was too busy to notice the approaching storm clouds.

Takini

Then he heard a rumble of thunder in the distance. Now he knew he had to prepare for bad weather.

Takini worked fast. He ran to a stack of driftwood which had been piled up during spring floods. He yanked the largest pole from the pile. He dropped the pole near the unconscious boy. Next Takini ran to Friendly and took his bridle and lead rope from the horse's neck. Using the bridle and braided rope, the boy lashed the pole to the two trees which stood about eight feet apart. He quickly began leaning more poles at an angle against the cross pole to fashion a lean-to shelter. From a spruce tree Takini snapped off many of the lower branches and began covering the lean-to frame. He knew how to place the branches so the needles would angle downward all in the same direction to shed rain.

Just as Takini placed the final branches on the lean-to, large drops of rain began to pelt the trees and bushes. After gently pulling the helpless boy into the lean-to, Takini raced to Friendly. The young horse stood in place patiently waiting for his master to return. The boy stroked Friendly's neck and rubbed his ears.

"Good boy, Friendly! You are a real friend! Now I need your help! Go home! Bring help! Go home! Go!"

Waving his arms toward the hill they had just come down, Takini gently slapped Friendly's rear. Just as if the colt understood every word, he galloped off toward the hill. Takini hurried back to the lean-to where he and Lone Dog crawled inside next to the lifeless boy.

"He's still breathing, Lone Dog. Maybe he has a chance to live. Maybe Friendly will bring help. We must stay. Wakan Tanka led us to this boy. He wants us to be here to care for this boy he created. Now lie down. The boy needs us."

Takini continued to sprinkle cool water on the boy's swollen forehead. He ignored his own hunger and thirst as many questions poured through his mind. *Will this boy live or die? Who is he? Is he from an enemy tribe? Will they come looking for him? When will Friendly return? Will our people pay any attention to the colt they never trusted? What if Friendly comes back alone, or what if he never comes back?*

Takini was sure it was up to him to stay no matter what happened. He was convinced the hawk was sent by Wakan Tanka to lead him to the injured boy. He knew Lone Dog was also part of the plan to bring him to the boy who would surely die without help. Takini never forgot his mother's words, "You will serve our people well. Wakan

83

Takini

Tanka will guide you. You will grow up to be a good and brave man."

Takini knew in his heart he was doing something good and brave. He was sure Wakan Tanka would protect him in all that he tried to do. He made up his mind that he would not leave this boy to die alone. All Takini could do now was care for the helpless boy and wait. He did not know at that very moment big trouble was already heading his way.

6
Captured

The pouring rain forced the Unkpapa people to stay in their lodges. Only a few young men and boys were outside, always spread out on the high ridges watching for any sign of approaching enemies. They could never let down their guard. A surprise attack could mean the death of many unsuspecting people. No chances could be taken, and the lookouts remained alert day and night.

On one of the highest ridges, a young warrior took shelter under a giant fir tree. Protected from the drenching rain, the young man scanned the surrounding valleys for any trouble. It was a quiet morning. Nothing was moving anywhere. Time passed slowly. Then there it was. Something was coming down a distant hillside. The lookout was sure it must be a horse. It was hard to see if the horse carried a rider.

The young man watched closely as the animal continued downhill. *What was a horse doing all alone on that hillside? Did it belong to an enemy soldier or warrior? Was a rider lying close to the horse's body to remain hidden from view?* The lookout would soon have the answers to his questions.

Finally the young man could relax. As the horse came closer, he could see this horse did not have a rider. Soon he thought he recognized this horse. *Could it be the crazy colt Takini had tamed and now called Friendly? Did the wild colt suddenly go beserk and throw the boy to the ground? What was this animal doing roaming the hills alone in the pouring rain?*

The lookout watched as Friendly galloped into the village. A woman, out gathering an arm load of firewood, hollered for someone to chase the colt out of the village. A young boy came out to see what was going on. Instantly he recognized Takini's horse and raced to Four Horns' lodge to give him the news. Four Horns told the boy to find Takini, and tell him to take care of Friendly. The man thought Takini was in Sitting Bull's lodge.

The boy could not find Takini anywhere. He was about to give up and go back to Four Horns' lodge and tell him, when another boy said he saw Takini ride Friendly north away from the village early that morning. Hearing the news, Four Horns decided to wait and see if Takini would come back on his own. Friendly was led from the village and taken to the place where the rest of the horses were grazing west of the village.

After the boy let Friendly loose, he raced back to the village to escape the pouring rain. As the boy reached the village, he was met by Friendly. The colt was deliberately blocking his path and stood pawing the ground with his left hoof.

"What are you doing back here?" the startled boy hollered. "Are you crazy?"

Takini

Four Horns heard all the commotion, grabbed a buffalo hide, put it over his head, and came out to investigate. He saw the boy standing in front of Friendly who still pawed at the ground. The boy explained how he had left Friendly with the other horses, and how the crazy colt beat him back to the village.

"Something's wrong," Four Horns proclaimed. "Where is the boy? Why did Friendly come back without Takini? The boy must be in some kind of trouble."

Four Horns hurried to Sitting Bull's lodge to ask about Takini. The chief told Four Horns that the boy had left to search for a location for his vision quest. Sitting Bull said the boy might be almost anywhere. The chief was sure the boy was all right.

"Four Horns, the boy will be back. Wakan Tanka will care for him. Takini has been blessed with special gifts and powerful medicine. He'll be back," the chief proclaimed.

If Sitting Bull could see what was coming toward Takini, the chief might not be so sure. Takini was in for a terrifying shock. As he sat next to the unconscious boy, Takini continued to clean the boy's wound. He applied cool water to the swelling on his forehead. Rain kept pouring down. The lean-to was shedding most of the water.

There were only a few bad leaks. As water came through the small openings, Takini was able to catch some in his waterbag. This saved him several trips to the creek. Lone Dog lay sound asleep at the injured boy's feet.

Suddenly the injured boy moved his head. Then his eyes slowly opened. The badly injured boy blinked and rubbed his eyes. One look around and his eyes filled with terror. The surprised Takini quickly used his hands to speak to the boy with sign language.

"Don't be afraid. I'm your friend. I will not hurt you. I am here to help you live."

The boy managed a weak smile and passed out again. All was strangely quiet except for the sound of rain hitting the roof of the shelter. Occasionally a faint sound of thunder rolled across the distant hills. Takini was startled when Lone Dog raised his head and growled.

"What is it, dog? Why do you growl? Has Friendly come back?"

Lone Dog suddenly jumped up and ran to the entrance of the lean-to growling and barking loudly.

"Lone Dog!'" shouted Takini. "Stop barking! Sit! Stay!"

Then it happened. A man rode his horse right up to the lean-to. Takini crawled from the shelter and stood next to his dog. Again the boy ordered Lone Dog to stop barking and to stay. This man was huge. He jumped from his horse and gave Takini a shove. The man crawled into the shelter and knelt next to his injured son. When he saw his son was still alive, the man came out of the shelter and stood facing Takini. In his Crow language the man began shouting at Takini. The boy understood nothing the man was saying, but he was sure the man thought he had hurt his son. With sign language Takini told the whole story of finding the boy and trying to help him.

Again the man shouted at Takini and grabbed him by the arm and forced him to sit on the ground in the soaking rain. The man tore two long poles from the lean-to. He quickly tied a pole to each side of his horse's saddle. He tied shorter poles across the two long poles to create a platform. The man took a buffalo hide from his horse and placed it over the platform. Takini watched as the man carefully lifted the unconscious boy onto the buffalo hide. After wrapping both sides of the hide over the boy, the man used hide rope to secure the boy to the travois.

Takini wondered what the man would do next. *Would he just ride off and leave him? Would he do something to hurt him?* Takini's questions were answered when the man

Takini is taken captive by Crow father.

grabbed his arm and yanked him to his feet. He shoved Takini toward his horse and motioned him to climb on. While Takini pulled himself to the horse's back, the man made one final check on his injured son and the travois. Suddenly Lone Dog began barking and charged at the man. The warrior kicked Lone Dog in the head. The poor dog howled in pain.

"Lone Dog, go! Go home!" Takini screamed.

Lone Dog crouched near the lean-to whimpering softly. Takini wished he could go over to his faithful dog and hug him, but the man jumped on his horse in front of Takini and signaled his horse to move. He held the horse back, making the animal move slowly so the travois would remain steady. The man constantly looked back to make sure the boy was comfortable. The horse successfully crossed the creek with the travois. Soon they were moving through the sagebrush and away from the creek.

Takini wondered what would happen next. *Would he be made a prisoner? Would these people kill him? Would he have a chance to escape? Where was Friendly? What would happen to Lone Dog? Would he ever see his animal friends and his people again? Would Wakan Tanka show him what to do?* All these questions poured through the boy's mind. He asked these questions silently over and over again. The boy could hardly believe these awful things were happening to him.

Takini stopped asking the questions and began planning an escape. He knew he would have to have a perfect plan. He would probably have only one chance. If he failed, he knew he would surely die. Takini's eyes examined every ridge, every stand of trees and bushes, and every landmark. If he did make an escape, he would have to know the route to travel to complete a successful escape.

The man guided his horse through the pouring rain and up over a low ridge. They crossed two more ridges when suddenly the man pulled his horse to a halt. The man jumped down and ran back to the injured boy. The lad was awake again. He managed to smile up at the man. The two of them talked softly. The man said nothing about Takini. He told the boy to rest, and they would be home soon.

The man mounted up, and they were soon on their way again. Then Takini saw an unbelievable sight! The boy's heart began pounding in his chest. There they were! A dog and a single horse were crossing a distant hillside. Takini knew immediately it had to be Lone Dog and Friendly. The boy was trembling with fear. He knew the warrior would not hesitate to kill Friendly and Lone Dog. Takini tried to look away so the man would not realize he had seen his animal friends.

"Stay back! Stay back!" the boy said to himself.

Almost like Friendly and Lone Dog had heard Takini, the two of them stopped next to a stand of spruce trees. When they disappeared into the dense trees, Takini breathed a sigh of relief. *Did the dog and the colt understand the danger? Were they smart enough to know they must keep out of sight?* He knew animals were very clever and understood more than anyone imagined they could. Takini knew Wakan Tanka would use his dog and his horse to help him. The hawk had been sent to lead Takini to the injured boy. Takini believed Wakan Tanka would never abandon him. He had faith that somehow he, Friendly, and Lone Dog would be safely back with their people.

Friendly and Lone Dog had stopped just in time.

Over the very next ridge, Takini looked down on a huge Crow village. There were at least forty lodges erected near a river. A large herd of horses grazed just west of the village. The rain had stopped, and the Crow people were out doing their work. When the Crow warrior approached the village, many people gathered around to find out what had happened. The man grabbed Takini by the arm and almost threw him to the ground. The boy was barely able to land on his feet. The warrior shouted for a man to take Takini away where he could be watched every minute.

As the man told the crowd his story, he carefully untied his son and gently laid him on the ground with the buffalo robe still protecting the injured boy. The boy was wide awake. He did not know Takini was a prisoner of his people. The injured boy immediately began telling his story. He said he remembered his horse stumbling in the creek, and the next thing he knew he was in a lean-to shelter with a strange boy and a dog. He described how the boy helped him, and how he tried to treat his injury. As soon as his son mentioned Takini, the man called to those guarding Takini. He was brought to the man and his son. The injured boy smiled and shouted something in the Crow language. Takini could not understand what the boy said. He didn't know the injured boy was telling everyone that Takini helped him and had saved his life.

The boy's father explained to his son, "This boy is Lakota! He is our enemy! Why would he want to help you, a Crow? He probably planned to take you to the Lakota camp and make you a slave! We can never trust the enemy!"

Takini

The boy told his father he was sure Takini was a friend and did not mean to do him any harm. He asked his father to let Takini go.

"My son, I am happy this Lakota boy helped you, but he is still our enemy. We will have to keep him here. He cannot go free. He will return and tell his people we are here. This cannot happen."

The injured boy frowned. He was not allowed to talk back to his father. When the boy looked at Takini, Takini could tell by the boy's expression that the Crow people would never let him go. Now he was sure that escape was the only answer. Every second Takini would be alert for the first chance to run. It would have to be the right moment. One mistake and Takini would be killed.

As Takini scanned the hills surrounding the village, he saw several good routes for his escape. While examining all the nearby hills, the boy's heart skipped a beat. He saw an amazing sight on the ridge directly south of the village. A warm feeling filled Takini's body.

There on the ridge stood a horse with a dog sitting next to it. A majestic hawk circled high above the two animals.

Could it be? thought Takini. *Yes, there they are! It's Friendly and Lone Dog and hawk!*

The boy wanted to signal for his two friends to leave before they were seen by the enemy. The Crow would surely capture or kill both of them if they knew they belonged to Takini. Suddenly Friendly turned and disappeared into the trees and Lone Dog followed him. Takini felt another sense of relief to see his friends out of sight of the enemy for now. He wondered what his animal friends would do next. *Could they understand the danger they faced? Was Friendly smart enough to know he had to stay hidden?* How Takini wished he could run up the ridge, jump on Friendly, and gallop away.

Takini knew he would never make it up the ridge to Friendly without being seen and recaptured or killed. The boy watched the hawk continue to glide in a circle directly over the ridge and the trees that hid Friendly and Lone Dog. Takini felt strangely calm. The boy was sure the hawk was Wakan Tanka's messenger and had come to help him. He could never explain these special feelings. He just knew that Wakan Tanka was with him every moment of his life. His mother said it would be that way.

Would Wakan Tanka bless Takini with another miracle? Would the Great Mystery lead him to freedom? The boy's questions would be answered very soon.

7
The Chase Is On

All afternoon, Takini kept his eyes on the clump of pine trees on the southern ridge. *Where were his animal friends? Were Friendly and Lone Dog still up there? What were they doing?* The boy worried that his animal friends would be seen and captured or killed. Even when the sun dropped below the western mountains, Takini saw no sign of Friendly or Lone Dog. The Crow men watched Takini every minute. The Crow leaders debated about what to do with the Lakota boy. Many argued that Takini should be put to death. Others said he should be made a slave. The injured boy begged his father to let Takini live. He kept telling his father how Takini had saved his life and deserved to live.

Takini had no idea about what was being discussed. All he could think about was his animal friends and if he would ever have a chance to escape. That night Takini was forced into a lodge where he would have to sleep surrounded by young enemy warriors. His route to the door of the lodge was completely blocked by sleeping Crow men. The boy couldn't sleep. His mind was racing with thoughts of escape and fear that his animal friends might be seen. He thought about Four Horns, Sitting Bull, and all the Unkpapa people he loved. His mind raced with thoughts of what might happen to him the next day.

When Takini finally fell asleep, he dreamed he had escaped and was running from his enemy. It seemed like he was numb and couldn't make his legs move fast enough. The harder he tried to run, the slower he went. This dream repeated itself over and over again.

A loud cracking sound suddenly startled the boy from a deep sleep. A Crow woman was snapping branches and dropping them on her fire just outside the lodge where Takini had been sleeping. The boy sat up rubbing his eyes. He noticed most of the young Crow warriors were already up and gone.

As Takini stood up, a man came into the lodge and grabbed him by the arm. He pulled the boy to the door and shoved him outside. The man signaled for Takini to get to work and help the woman break up the firewood into small lengths. Takini went right to work, and he quickly looked up at the ridge for any glimpse of Friendly or Lone Dog. They were nowhere to be seen.

After working for the woman for almost an hour, Takini was finally given a pemican cake and a little dried meat for his breakfast. As he ate, dark clouds began moving in from the west. *Was Wakan Tanka sending a storm to help him escape? Would he somehow find a way to escape in broad daylight?* The determined boy was ready to run at the first good chance to escape.

Takini

When Takini had all the wood broken into the right lengths, the man who shoved him from the lodge returned. He ordered Takini to walk with him to his horse which was tied near his teepee. When they reached the man's horse, with one sudden motion, the warrior lifted the boy onto the horse and jumped on behind him. Next two men rode up, one on each side of the horse where Takini sat with the warrior. After a few brief words, the three men began to ride toward the edge of the village.

Takini was confused. He wondered where they were taking him. He didn't understand why three men were escorting him away from the village. He feared the worst was about to happen and was sure they planned take him out of sight of the village to kill him. At the edge of the village, the warriors passed the injured boy who lay resting on a buffalo robe. The boy sat up and looked directly at the boy who had saved him. Takini saw a look of anger and sadness in the injured boy's eyes. Now Takini was positive the men had something horrible planned for him. He knew something would have to happen soon, or he would never live to see his people again.

Takini was right. The men intended to kill him, leave his body for the wild animals to devour, and return to their village knowing the Lakota boy would never be a problem for them. He would be one less enemy to worry about. The boy's final minutes were ticking away, he was outnumbered three to one, and had no weapon. It would take a miracle from Wakan Tanka to save him now. Takini looked to the heavens and said a prayer for a miracle to happen.

As the men rode away from the village, Takini had another worry. They were headed up the ridge straight toward the trees where Friendly and Lone Dog had disappeared the day before. *Would they find and kill Friendly and Lone Dog? Had the two animals left?* Takini frantically looked for any signs of movement in the trees above him. Suddenly there it was. The majestic hawk came gliding over the trees on the ridge. The hawk dipped down in a long swoop coming amazingly close to the warriors. Their horses began prancing and whinnying but quickly calmed down when the hawk flew away.

Takini's eyes were glued to the amazing bird. He was filled with excitement. Wakan Tanka's messenger had come to show him a way to escape! The boy was sure another miracle was about to happen. One of the warriors suddenly began talking loudly, and the man was pointing at the approaching storm. Another man began shouting. The men agreed to pass by the pine trees, drop into the next valley, quickly kill Takini, and get back to their village before the storm hit.

The men rode single file up to the pine trees. Takini was riding with the second warrior who had one arm holding him firmly. The first rider was about to meet with disaster. There, hiding in the trees a large dog crouched, waiting and ready to attack. With the first rider only a few feet away, Lone Dog let out a blood-curdling howl and bolted toward the first horse. The big dog sank his teeth into the horse's leg and tore its hide open. The huge animal reared up on its hind legs tossing its rider backward to the earth. Lone Dog was already sinking his teeth into the second horse carrying Takini and the man sitting behind him. The second horse went beserk and bucked Takini and the man into the air.

As soon as Takini hit the ground, he was up and running for his life. After running only fifty feet, a horse bolted from the trees in front of the startled boy.

"Friendly! It's you!" shrieked Takini.

With a tremendous leap, the boy was on Friendly's back and galloping away. One glance back and Takini was hor-

Lone Dog sinks his teeth into the leg of the warrior's horse.

rified to see the third man coming full speed to catch him. The terrified boy urged Friendly to gallop as fast as possible. Takini held his head down next to his horse's neck, shouting for Friendly to run like he had never done before. Lone Dog had not given up. He was in fast pursuit and raced up next to the third man's speeding horse watching for a chance to sink his teeth into its leg. The flying hooves made this impossible for the dog to accomplish without being kicked.

With a bigger and stronger horse, the warrior was quickly gaining on Takini. The man was riding the fastest horse in the Crow herd. The boy did not have a chance. No matter how hard Friendly tried, he could never outrun such a powerful and speedy horse. Takini continued to urge Friendly to go faster and faster, but the small horse had little more to give.

With the enemy warrior only twenty feet behind him, Takini flew past a dead tree which towered above him into the sky. A split second before the enemy warrior reached the dead tree, a bolt of lightning exploded toward the ground. The lightning bolt blasted the tree apart, causing it to come crashing to the earth right in front of the warrior's speeding horse. The poor animal had no time to stop. Its front legs hit the tree. The horse sprawled on the ground. The warrior went flying forward, striking his head as he landed on the rocky ground. He was knocked unconscious.

Miracles kept coming in the nick of time to give Takini his chance to escape. The boy and Friendly raced away, not knowing the other two riders had caught their horses and were on their way to find their friend and recapture Takini. The men were not giving up, and the boy was still in great danger.

Takini rode Friendly down hill toward a meandering river. Lone Dog did his best to keep up. The weary dog's tongue was hanging from the side of his mouth. When they reached the river, the boy directed his faithful horse into the shallow water. He slowed Friendly to a walk to move upstream for almost a mile. His plan was to leave no tracks for the enemy to follow. Takini was sure the men would attempt to find him and complete their mission to end his life.

The two warriors finally found their friend. The man lay unconscious and badly injured. One man stayed to help his fallen companion. The third man galloped on, following Friendly's tracks on the damp ground. He was sure he would soon succeed in tracking the boy down and make him pay for all the trouble he had caused.

The warrior easily tracked Friendly and Takini to the river. In the pouring rain the man reined his mount to a stop at the river's edge. He saw Friendly's tracks lead down to the water. He signaled his horse to enter the water and cross the stream. After reaching the opposite shore, the man searched for Friendly's tracks leading away from the river. There were none. He knew what Takini had done. Riding in the water was an old trick used to make a trail disappear.

The warrior looked up and down stream for any sign of Takini and his horse. Seeing nothing, the warrior sent his horse into a gallop along the riverbank heading downstream. All along the man examined the river bank for any signs of a horse leaving the stream. He rode a mile and a half without seeing a single sign. He turned his horse back upstream. Suddenly he heard a high-pitched scream coming from the direction of his injured friend. There on the ridge his friend was signaling for the man to stop the search and return. The news was not good. The unconscious warrior had died from his head injuries.

The two surviving warriors decided to take their dead friend back to their village and report to their elders. As

soon as they completed their sad journey, they planned to
return with more warriors, find Takini, and finish their
mission. They were full of great anger and determined to
seek revenge. Now, more than ever, they wanted to find
the Lakota boy and make him pay for the death of their
friend.

When Takini and Friendly finally left the river, they
moved on in the drenching rain. The boy had to slow
Friendly to a walk so Lone Dog could keep up. Takini
decided he would not take a direct route back to his people and lead the enemy to his people. He made up his
mind he would rather die first. He had no idea where his
enemy had gone or what they planned to do next. He had
no way of knowing that twenty warriors had painted on
their war colors, and were already on their way, determined to find him.

The rain was finally coming to an end and the lightning
and thunder had moved east. The storm was almost over.
Due east Takini saw a high hill. The northeast side was
covered with a dense forest of pine and spruce trees. The
boy smiled when he looked up and saw the hawk flying
above the hill. He was sure the hawk was telling him these
trees and this hill were there to help him escape. Without

hesitating, Takini rode Friendly straight for the trees. The trees would swallow him from view. No one would be able to see him as he made his way up the hill in the dense trees.

At the edge of the thick forest, Takini immediately found a game trail made by moose, elk, and deer. It would be the perfect route to follow. As the boy rode Friendly into the trees, he jumped down. The trail was so narrow, the only way through the forest would be to lead Friendly along this narrow trail. The boy had just entered the trees, when suddenly Lone Dog began growling.

"Quiet, Lone Dog!" whispered Takini. "What is it? Why do you growl? What are you trying to tell me?"

The boy moved back to the edge of the trees for a look. He was stunned by what he saw. There in the valley he had just left, stood twenty horses with twenty riders. One man was down on one knee next to his horse carefully examining the ground. Seconds later the man jumped to his feet and pointed right at the trees where Takini was hiding. The warrior jumped on his horse, and let out a blood-curdling cry, and galloped straight at Takini's hiding place. The other nineteen men screamed terrifying war cries and kicked their horses into full gallop.

Fear gripped Takini. His heart pounded wildly. *How would he ever escape so many warriors? Had the hawk come with the wrong message?* The boy moved swiftly, grabbing Friendly's lead rope, and he charged up the game trail as fast as humanly possible. He realized the warriors would reach the trees in no time. *Would they follow him, or would they go around and meet him coming out of the trees on top of the hill?*

No matter what happened, the boy had to trust Wakan Tanka to deliver him from these twenty warriors determined to seek their revenge and end his life in some horrible way. Takini was ready to run until the last of his strength was gone, then he would run some more. *If he could only get out of the trees before being caught, then maybe his faithful horse and brave dog could do the rest. Could there be another miracle ready to happen to help him overcome the twenty-to-one odds he was facing?* There was no time to think about anything but the next step toward freedom.

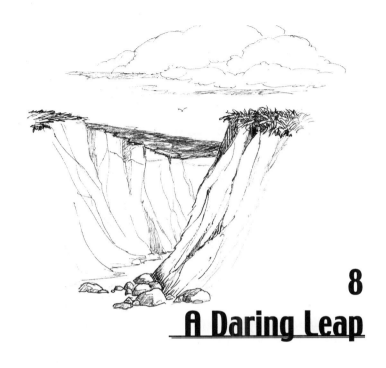

8
A Daring Leap

Takini ran faster than he had ever run before. The adrenaline was surging through his veins and arteries. He was gasping for every breath. Friendly followed, crashing through the trees, breaking dead branches, and staying close behind Takini. Lone Dog was nowhere to be seen. The boy could only hope his faithful dog would somehow make an escape on his own. There was nothing Takini could do to help his good friend.

Takini

As Takini charged up the game trail, suddenly he heard Lone Dog barking wildly. The big dog was behind him, charging in and out and around the first warrior's horse causing the animal to stop and kick at the bothersome dog. This slowed the first man down and caused all the warriors following to slow down at the same time. Suddenly a shot rang out followed by a tragic cry from Lone Dog.

"Lone Dog!" cried Takini. "My good friend, they shot you!"

Now it was harder than ever for the frantic boy to keep running, but he had no choice. *Was Lone Dog dead? Had Takini's faithful dog given his life to save his master?* Takini was filled with anger and hate.

"Those cowards have killed my dog!" the boy hollered.

Only minutes later everything changed. Takini heard barking again.

"Lone Dog! You're alive. Come! Don't give the cowards another shot at you! Come! We can get away together!" Takini screamed.

Takini felt completely helpless. He could not stop to help his friend. He wondered where the bullet had struck the poor dog. *Would he bleed to death from the wound?*

What can I do to help him? I can't stop, even one second! The men were still plowing through the trees leading their horses on as fast as possible. Something would have to happen soon or Takini would never live to see the dawn of another day.

Lone Dog had managed to slow the warriors just long enough for Takini to reach the top of the hill. As he led Friendly from the trees, Lone Dog came charging up. Takini could see no sign of an injury and no limp. The dog seemed to be in perfect shape. Takini jumped onto Friendly and galloped away from the trees. When Lone Dog passed Friendly, the boy spotted the dog's injury. Eight inches of Lone Dog's tail was dangling toward the earth. The warrior's bullet had severed the poor dog's tail, leaving only a thin strand of skin from which the end of his tail was hanging downward. Takini was thankful the bullet had not struck his dog in a fatal place. The tail would heal.

Friendly was galloping at full speed as Takini frantically searched for a way to make his escape. The warriors were already coming out of the trees and jumping on their horses. They would catch or shoot Takini in only a matter of minutes. Suddenly, along the ridge just southeast of the boy and his horse, the majestic hawk circled close to the ground. Why was the hawk flying there? Takini could see no sign of a place to escape in that direction. Takini realized he had no choice. He knew the graceful bird was his only hope. The hawk had always come when Takini needed Wakan Tanka's help. His messenger must have a reason for him to head in that direction. With the warriors coming at full speed, Takini turned Friendly toward the soaring hawk. His small horse was giving every ounce of energy and speed he had to save his master.

Where was an escape route? There was no place in sight where the boy, his dog, and his horse could hide. Just as Takini was thinking the hawk had led him in the wrong direction, there it was! Only fifty feet away was a sudden drop-off. A creek had carved a gorge sixty-feet deep into the land. Friendly didn't seem to see the drop-off. He continued to gallop at full speed toward the crack in the earth. Takini was tempted to rein Friendly to a stop before they both crashed to their deaths at the bottom of the gorge. A sudden calmness came over the boy telling him to just hang on and let Friendly go for it.

With the drop-off only fifteen feet away, Takini could hear the war cries of the twenty warriors speeding toward him. At the edge of the gorge the boy closed his eyes and hung on. Friendly never broke his stride, never slowed down. The small horse reached the edge of the chasm and launched himself into the air. In a spectacular leap, Friendly flew toward the other side of the deep ravine. Takini felt a tremendous jolt and almost went flying over his horse's head. Only his arms wrapped around Friendly's neck kept the boy from being catapulted into the ground.

Friendly's front hooves hit the edge of the gorge, but his back hooves didn't quite make it. Only a small ledge three feet down kept the horse from sliding backward into the sixty-foot drop. Friendly dug in with his front hooves while his rear hooves thrashed against the rock for leverage. Miraculously the small horse finally struggled to a standing position on solid ground. Instantly the boy and his horse headed away from the gorge.

"Friendly! You did it! You saved my life! You're amazing!"

As Takini praised his courageous horse, the enemy warriors came charging up to the edge of the gorge. Immediately their horses reared up, refusing to attempt the jump. Several of the angry warriors jumped from their horses and began shooting at Takini, but the boy was already out of range. One warrior was preparing to go back

Friendly makes a spectacular leap over a deep ravine.

with his horse and with a running start try to jump the gorge. His leader shouted at the man, telling him to stop. The leader said no more men would die because of this boy. The lead warrior believed the boy must have a powerful guardian spirit and ordered the men to turn back.

When the twenty warriors returned to their village, all of them were talking about the unbelievable jump made by such a small horse. Many believed the Great Spirit had given the little horse wings.

As Takini rode away, he suddenly had a sinking feeling. *Where was Lone Dog?* The boy hadn't seen his brave dog since they had left the trees. *Had the warriors finally killed the brave dog?* Takini wished he could go back to look for the dog who had saved his life. All the boy could do was ask Wakan Tanka to watch over his friend and help Lone Dog make it back alive.

Takini rode Friendly down a hill so steep he had to guide his horse on an angle across the precipitous slope. He had to lean back to keep from sliding forward over Friendly's head. The boy trusted his good friend to keep his footing and make it to the bottom safely. Friendly was trained well and could handle almost any terrain, and soon they reached the meadow below the steep hill. Takini directed Friendly straight for the tall willows on the edge of the field. Soon they had disappeared from view.

With no sign of Lone Dog, Takini had an empty feeling. *Had the brave dog given his life for his master? Would Takini ever know what happened to his good friend?* The boy's heart ached. He remembered how Lone Dog had fearlessly charged the enemy horses, sinking his teeth into their legs and causing them to throw their riders. He remembered how Lone Dog had harassed the horses in the trees slowing the men, giving him a chance to escape. Takini wished he could give his dog a hug and thank him for saving his life.

The heavyhearted boy rode Friendly into an opening surrounded by willow bushes. He stopped to give his weary friend a rest. When Takini's feet hit the ground, he stood very still staring into the clear blue sky. He seemed to be in a trance. High above soared the graceful hawk. The boy's mind went back to the day the Lakota hunters found him with his dying mother. That was the first day the hawk came to glide in great circles above his teepee. It was the day he begged the great bird to bring help. He remembered how the magnificent hawk had dipped its wing like it was trying to send him a message. Now, amaz-

ingly, this hawk came diving in a powerful swoop flutter-
ing one wing exactly like the first hawk had done.

"What are you telling me, kind messenger?" cried
Takini. "O winged friend, are you here to help me again?
I need your help! Please lead me to Lone Dog! Please help
me find him!"

After gliding over the boy in one more great circle, the
majestic hawk turned and soared away. Takini realized he
was alone and not safe yet. No more precious time could
be wasted. The warriors could have found a way around
the gorge and might be on their way to find him at this
very moment. If they ever caught him, Takini knew it
would cost both him and his faithful horse their lives.
When Takini rode into the willows, he was quite sure there
had to be water nearby. Willows like and need water.

The boy was right. He found a shallow creek twisting
its way through the willows. Takini took time to let
Friendly have a good drink of the refreshing water. The
liquid would renew his strength. The boy planned to ride
Friendly upstream for a long distance. It was another
chance to travel without tracks for the enemy to follow.
He planned to find a rocky place where Friendly could
leave the creek without leaving telltale tracks.

Takini

Up the creek they walked, well hidden by thick willows. Takini became more and more worried about Lone Dog. *Where could he be all this time?* It did not look good. After only thirty minutes, which really seemed like hours, about ninety feet ahead Takini saw the perfect place to leave the creek. Rounded rocks left by an ancient glacier filled a dry drainage. Friendly was soon stepping carefully through the loose rock. He had to be careful not to slip or stumble.

"Good horse! Friendly, you are still saving me from the enemy! Keep going, boy! We can make it! I will tell our people you are the greatest the horse our Lakota people have ever seen."

Friendly turned his ears back toward Takini as if he was trying to catch the boy's every word. Takini felt in his heart that his trusty horse understood every word he spoke. The boy only wished Lone Dog could be there to hear all the things he wanted to say to his brave canine. Takini thought about the mighty hawk. *Could the great bird understand his words, too? Could the hawk somehow help Lone Dog? Would Wakan Tanka answer his prayers for the safety of Lone Dog?* Takini believed nothing was impossible for the Great Mystery. He still had hope that one day he see his Lone Dog again.

After leaving the creek and riding through trees and bushes at the base of a hill, Takini suddenly realized the day was nearly over. Soon darkness would envelop the land. The boy was very hungry. Friendly needed time to graze. They would not find their people before nightfall and would soon need a good place to spend the night. The trees were blocking the boy's view of the surrounding area. Takini turned Friendly south and came out onto a gentle hillside. There, with daylight time running out, he spotted the perfect place to spend the night. Not far ahead were at least a dozen giant spruce trees. They would make the perfect hiding place. Next to the spruce trees there was plenty of good grass for Friendly.

The sun was already down when Takini reached the trees. He slid from Friendly's back and stood near the great trees. The boy slipped the bridle from his exhausted horse's head and let him begin to enjoy his fill of sweet grasses. Takini stood for a few minutes stroking Friendly's neck and back.

"Good horse. You saved my life. I will take care of you. We will soon be back to our people. Now you can eat and rest. There is no horse better than you. Wakan Tanka gave me the greatest horse ever."

Takini

As Takini watched Friendly slowly move away to graze, the boy saw an awful sight. The inside of his horse's hind legs had been scraped raw. Lines of blood oozed from the deep scrapes. When Friendly had jumped the gorge, his hind legs hit the edge of the chasm. As Friendly kicked wildly to get a hold and keep from falling backward into the ravine, he tore the hide from his legs. His injuries were caused by the heroic effort to carry his master to safety and freedom. Takini felt sick. He understood what his faithful horse had done to save him from certain death. He walked over to Friendly and threw his arms around the small horse's neck.

"Friendly, you're hurt! You were hurt saving my life! When we find our people there will be medicine to help you heal. Four Horns will know what to do. Everyone will hear what you did to save my life. No other horse could do what you have done."

Takini wrapped hide around his horse's injured legs, gave Friendly a final hug, walked to a huge spruce tree, and crawled under its low hanging branches. Completely exhausted, he lay down on a soft mattress of grass he had laid over a bed of fallen needles. He began thinking about all that had happened during the last two days. Takini's heart ached for Lone Dog. Like Friendly, Lone Dog did his part to save Takini's life. Now his fantastic dog was gone. *Had the cowardly enemy taken their revenge out on Lone Dog? Had the faithful dog given his life for Takini?* The boy could only pray that Wakan Tanka would provide one more miracle and allow Lone Dog to survive and come home. The answer to Takini's prayers was on the way.

9
A Race for Life

Takini lay awake far into the night. Many thoughts raced through his mind. As hard as he tried, he could not fall asleep. He rolled and tossed for hours. When sleep finally came, it was a restless sleep full of many dreams. Worst of all was the dream of seeing Lone Dog running for his life with enemy warriors all around him. An enemy warrior rode up to Lone Dog with the largest rifle Takini

127

had ever seen. The heartless man shot and killed the help-less dog.

It was during one of these nightmares that Takini thought he felt something rubbing against his back. He didn't dare move. *What could this be? Was it a wild animal? Was it a porcupine full of sharp quills?* A groggy Takini froze in fear, not daring to move. Another miracle happened just seconds later. A rough tongue was licking the boy's face. Takini sat upright and put his hand out. *Could it be true? Yes, it was!* Lone Dog had returned.

"Lone Dog! It's you! You're alive! How did you do it? Wakan Tanka brought you back to me! Now we are all together! We will all make it back to our people! Nothing can stop us now!" Takini wrapped his arms around Lone Dog giving him a hug. "Lie down. Tomorrow we will find our people. They will hear about you, and how you charged the enemy horses and saved me from certain death."

Takini saw that Lone Dog's tail was already healing well. The loose end had fallen off, and the bleeding had stopped. With his arms around Lone Dog's neck, the boy settled back onto his mattress. He was the happiest boy on earth. His animal friends had helped him escape a deter-mined and powerful enemy. Quietly Takini thanked

128

Wakan Tanka for saving their lives and for allowing Lone Dog to come back. Now he prayed he and his friends could leave their enemies far behind and return to their people. He thanked Wakan Tanka for the hawk he had sent to help them. Takini wondered if the hawk had somehow helped Lone Dog. *Was the hawk truly a messenger sent by Wakan Tanka?* Takini was sure it had to be true.

As Friendly grazed nearby, Takini curled up next to Lone Dog and both fell into a deep sleep. Now the boy's dreams changed. In one dream he watched as all twenty enemy warriors fell into the gorge to their deaths. In the same dream Friendly jumped a chasm so wide that the little horse had to use his legs to fly. When daylight finally came, Takini woke up shivering, stiff, and sore. Lone Dog had already left to get a drink from the creek. The boy reached the creek as Lone Dog was climbing the bank.

"Good dog," the boy whispered as he dropped to his knees giving his faithful dog a hug. "Water is good for you. I wish I had food to give you. When we find our people, I will give you all the delicious buffalo meat you can eat. You are the best dog on our mother earth."

Takini found a place where the grassy bank sloped down to the water. He was able to lie on the bank, put his face right into the water, and drink lots of the delicious liquid. He was weak from lack of food, and the water revived him a little. When he stood after his drink, Takini felt dizzy and woozy. He needed food desperately. Service berries alone were not enough to give the hungry boy the strength he needed to keep going.

With Lone Dog at his side, Takini hurried to find Friendly. His trusty horse looked up when he heard the boy coming. Takini removed the hide bandages from his horse's legs and examined them. They were already beginning to heal. A little blood still oozed from some of the deepest cuts. Friendly turned his head and nuzzled the boy with his damp nose.

"Good boy, Friendly. You are doing better. It's time to go and find our people. We can do it. Nothing can stop us now. Let's go!"

Takini quickly slipped the hide bridle over Friendly's neck. With a graceful move, the boy mounted his faithful horse and rode into the trees with Lone Dog trailing behind. It wouldn't be hard to find his people's old camp, but Takini knew they wouldn't be there. He had been gone for three days and was sure his people had moved by now.

130

All that day the boy, his horse, and his dog traveled on a course which kept them hidden from view. Takini never stayed in an open area for more than a few minutes. He wanted to take no chances. Weak from hunger, the boy thought about getting back to his people and enjoying some delicious food. His imagination was so good, he thought he could smell buffalo meat roasting. Takini stopped at every stream to drink his fill of refreshing water.

It was late in the afternoon when Takini recognized the ridge which rose above his people's camp. He knew he was almost there. Friendly steadily climbed the hill and carried Takini to the crest of the ridge. He looked in every direction to make sure no one was following him. The boy was disappointed to look down and see his people had left. This was expected and would not stop him. He couldn't give up and must keep going. The dejected boy directed Friendly down the hill and into the abandoned camp.

Takini didn't know it, but many of his people thought he would never return. They were sure something horrible had happened to the boy they called *Survivor*. Sitting Bull told the people they were wrong to think such thoughts. The great chief predicted that Takini would return and that Wakan Tanka was taking care of him. Even when searchers came back without being able to find the boy, the chief still refused to believe Takini was not coming back. Sitting Bull was so sure Takini was going to return, the chief asked his wife to hang cooked buffalo roasts from the branch of a tree where no animal could reach them. He predicted that Takini would return to this place looking for his people, pick up their trail, and follow it home.

"This food is for the boy. He will come by this place. He will be hungry. He will know we are waiting for him to come back to us. Takini will return!" Sitting Bull proclaimed.

Several men and women thought it was a waste of good buffalo meat, but they did not dare say what they thought. No one wanted to speak against the great chief. They still believed the boy would never be able to find his way back and never take even one bite of this meat.

As Takini rode Friendly through the abandoned camp suddenly Lone Dog dashed to the edge of the village and began barking. Lone Dog stood under a tree, looking up, wagging his tail wildly, and barking loudly.

"Quiet!" Takini shouted. "Why are you barking? Is there a bear in the tree?"

When Takini and Friendly reached the tree at the edge of the camp, the boy could see why Lone Dog was so

Lone Dog finds meat left for Takini.

excited. He could hardly believe his eyes. There hanging from a limb were large slabs of buffalo roast. It was the most delicious surprise the boy had ever seen. It didn't take long for Takini to get the meat down. With a long pole, he lifted the hide strap holding the meat and jiggled it up and down. In less than two minutes the hide loosened, and the meat dropped into Takini's hands. One look at the meat and the boy had more good news. This meat was quite fresh. It must have been left hanging on the tree that very morning. The meat was not one bit dried out.

Takini could have danced with joy. He had food, his people were not far away, and he was on their trail. He looked up at the blue sky and silently thanked Wakan Tanka for being so good to him. He was sure this delicious food was left just for him. He knew his people still believed he would return to them. He slid off Friendly and before eating a bite himself, the starving boy gave his faithful dog two large pieces of meat. Lone Dog's tail was wagging faster than ever. The dog made quick work of the meat. Takini immediately stuffed the rest of the meat into his food bag and climbed on Friendly. He would eat his first strips of meat while he moved on down the trail.

The buffalo roast was the finest meat Takini had ever tasted. He chewed it slowly, enjoying every mouthful. His mood had changed so fast. One minute he was starving, disappointed, and alone. The next minute he had food, knew his people were close, and he had a trail to follow.

"Friendly, I know you are hungry, too. Soon we will find good grass and a good place to camp. Tomorrow we will find our people."

Friendly, Lone Dog, and Takini were heading west on the trail their people had made. Takini was the happiest boy on earth, but he knew time was getting short. Soon this day would end. He planned to leave the trail and find a safe place to spend the night. He did not want to be too close to the trail which the enemy might find and follow. He wanted to be near a place where there would be plenty of grass for Friendly and where the enemy could not easily find him.

With the sun already down, Takini rode Friendly over a low ridge into a beautiful meadow. On the side of this open field a stand of dense trees was just what the boy was looking for. It would serve as a great place to hide for the night. A few minutes later Takini and Friendly reached the edge of the forest. The boy slid to the ground, removed Friendly's bridle, and rubbed the faithful horse's ears.

"This is good grass. Time for Friendly to eat," declared Takini as he patted Friendly's backside and let him begin grazing.

The tired boy walked to a place where the bushes and trees were the thickest. He pushed his way into bushes and trees where he would be completely out of sight of any enemy who might come into the meadow. He was sure Friendly could make his escape from any enemy who came his way.

Lone Dog followed Takini into the dense growth, and the two of them sat huddled together. They both enjoyed some more delicious buffalo roast. Takini was grateful to Wakan Tanka and to his people for helping him through all his troubles. He thought many times about the majestic hawk and all the help the great bird had given him. He was sure Wakan Tanka's spirit lived in the beautiful creature which came to help him so many times.

Another long restless night lay ahead, but the boy was sure he would find his people the very next day. They couldn't be too far away. They would have to stop early to set up their camp. Takini was confident his ordeal would be over soon. He had no way of knowing the next day would be far from easy or safe. Another threat to his life was on the way.

The night seemed endless. Takini curled up next to Lone Dog. The two friends lay on the bed of needles which had fallen from the pine trees. The boy slept for only a few fitful hours and woke up stiff and groggy. After eating some meat and sharing some with Lone Dog, the boy called Friendly, mounted up, and rode off toward his people's trail. Lone Dog was frisky and excited to be moving again. Friendly's legs were healing well. The boy was looking forward to getting back to his people soon.

Takini guided Friendly west and on an angle toward the wide trail his people had left. Warm rays of the sun had just touched the boy and his horse as they reached the crest of a hill. The boy smiled as he caught sight of his people's trail in the valley only a short distance below him. The hill sloped gently west parallel to the wide trail. For some unknown reason something was seeming to tell the boy to stay off the trail. Instead of riding Friendly straight down to the trail, Takini decided to stay on the sloping hill and remain away from the trail. The boy had a strange feeling the trail was a dangerous place to be. It was almost like Wakan Tanka was telling him that disaster waited on that trail.

Reaching a low place on the slope, Takini turned Friendly toward some massive boulders which were very close to the wide trail. As they rounded the last huge boulder, Lone Dog suddenly ran directly in front of Friendly. The boy reined his horse to a stop before Lone Dog was stepped on by Friendly. The frantic dog raced wildly in small circles in front of the startled horse.

"What's wrong with that dog?" Takini wondered. *"What is Lone Dog trying to tell us?"*

The boy quickly jumped to the ground. He was sure Lone Dog had seen something on the other side of this final boulder. *What could it be? Was it a great bear, enemy warriors, or soldiers? Takini's heart was pounding. Could something go wrong now, when he was so close to his people?* Takini could not take any chances. He was sure Lone Dog was trying to tell him he was in great danger.

The shaken boy hurriedly tied Friendly to a small tree and signaled his horse to stay. Takini worked his way between two boulders, squeezing through a very narrow space. When he reached an opening between the boulders, he stopped instantly. The trail was only a hundred feet away. Through the narrow opening Takini could see only a small section of the well-beaten trail. He could see nothing unusual. Then Lone Dog began to growl softly. The boy moved forward inch-by-inch for a better look. Suddenly Takini stopped, paralyzed by what he saw. Something was moving just inside the aspen trees lining the far side of the trail. "Soldiers! Two soldiers!" he whispered as he pulled back. His heart was pounding in his throat.

"They're after my people! They will find my people before I do! I have to get out of here! I have to let my people know these soldiers are tracking them!"

Takini had to think fast. He had to find a way to get back to his people without wasting a second and without being seen. He hurried through the boulders to Friendly. He untied his horse, mounted, and rode away from the boulders and the trail. With the hill between him and the trail, Takini turned Friendly west. Hopefully the soldiers would continue their slow pace. That would give the boy the chance to put distance between him and the enemy bluecoats.

When he was sure he was far ahead of the soldiers, Takini turned Friendly toward the trail to check on the soldiers. They were nowhere in sight. After hurrying on and checking the trail two more times, the boy signaled Friendly to stop. His horse was lathered up and breathing very hard. This was a welcomed rest for a weary animal. As the boy stroked Friendly's sweating shoulders, he heard a loud screeching cry. Looking high above him, Takini saw the graceful hawk gliding in wide circles.

"There you are again!" whispered Takini. "Did Wakan Tanka send you to help me again? I know you have come with good news! Thank you for coming to bring me joy! Let's go, Friendly! Come on, Lone Dog! Hawk is here to lead us!"

With the amazing hawk flying in the distance, Takini urged Friendly to go at top speed. Lone Dog did his best to keep up with the galloping horse. The boy was careful to stay out of sight of the trail. Several times he stopped, crawled on his stomach, and checked the trail for danger. Everytime he stopped, the hawk came swooping down toward him as if to say, "Why are you stopping? I'm not stopping!"

Finally Takini seemed to get the message. He didn't stop again. On he rode with his weary horse doing his best to keep going at top speed. Lone Dog trailed a short distance behind with his tongue dangling from the side of his mouth. Takini wondered how much longer it would take to reach his people. Friendly could not continue at this pace much longer. The boy did not want his faithful horse to die of exhaustion. Still he had to find his people and warn them of the danger. The soldiers could not be very far away.

10
A Great Vision

Takini had not seen the hawk for a long time. As he moved to a place where he could see the trail one last time, he saw the great bird flying very close to the ground. It was gliding in very small circles as if it was trying hard to make sure Takini was watching. Standing between two tall pine trees so he would be hard to see, Takini stared intently at the beautiful hawk. Suddenly the hawk flew lower than ever and very close to Takini. Then the great bird soared up and away. The boy watched the hawk fly west to a place where the wide trail crossed a small hill. When the hawk reached the top of the low rise, it landed on the limb of a huge dead tree. The bird stretched tall, flapped its wings, and sat as still as a statue.

Takini knew he must head for that hill. The hawk was telling him he needed to come to that spot. He was sure he understood the message the hawk had given him. The boy ordered Friendly to stay in the trees where they couldn't be seen. He planned to remain in the trees and follow them to the base of the hill. Only then would Takini leave the trees and head uphill to the spot where the hawk was perched.

What was the hawk's message this time? What was on the other side of the hill? Takini hoped and prayed he would see his people below on the other side. Takini guided Friendly slowly through the protective trees. As he reached the bottom of the hill, Takini thought he smelled smoke. The young boy's heart pounded with excitement. The smoke must mean his people were camped nearby. Still he could not take any chances. He would not show himself until he was sure he had found his people. It was possible enemies were camped nearby.

Finally, very close to the trail, Takini slid off Friendly's back. He rubbed his horse's neck as he looped the reins

The hawk sends Takini another message.

around a sturdy tree and signaled Lone Dog to stay by his side. Boy and dog moved slowly and silently up the hill toward the hawk's perch.

"O mighty hawk! Have you come to help me again? Have you led me to my people? Were you sent by Wakan Tanka to help me?" whispered Takini. Hope filled his heart. As he reached the hawk's tree, Takini looked up at his majestic friend. Amazingly the great bird stared directly at the boy. When their eyes met, Takini tingled with a wonderful sensation. He felt like he was being lifted from the ground and was gliding through the air as he had seen the hawk do many times. The boy stood frozen in one place like he was in a trance. He couldn't take his eyes from the piercing eyes of this beautiful bird.

Suddenly Takini was startled by the crack of a dead branch. Instantly the boy dropped to his knees and scrambled on all fours into some nearby bushes. He wondered why Lone Dog wasn't growling. Then he realized Lone Dog was nowhere to be seen. *What was going on? Where had his dog gone?* Suddenly another loud crack rang in Takini's ears. Then Lone Dog could be heard barking and a familiar voice began calling Lone Dog's name. Takini could not believe his ears. He knew the voice. It was Gray Feather, a girl his same age. The boy jumped up and called for Lone Dog to come.

"Takini! Is that you? I'm over here!" Gray Feather called.

He ran toward the sound of the girl's voice. He broke from the dense trees into a small opening. There she was. Gray Feather was standing near a pile of firewood she had gathered for her family.

"Takini! I'm so happy you are alive! Our great chief said Wakan Tanka would take care of you. The wise Sitting Bull even had meat left in a tree to help you come back alive!"

The boy could not speak. He just stood there listening to the wonderful voice of this beautiful girl. Gray Feather's words were a thrill to hear. Takini finally started talking. As fast as possible, he explained the scary time he had during the last few days.

"I can't talk much now. I have to go get Friendly. I'll be right back."

"I'll go with you!" shouted Gray Feather. "I love your horse! You have changed the horse everyone hated into one of the best horses ever! Friendly loves you!"

As they walked through the trees, Takini told Gray Feather how Friendly had injured his legs when he jumped the gorge. The girl cringed as Takini described how the hide was torn from Friendly's hind legs.

"Friendly saved your life. I know he will do anything for you. Four Horns will help Friendly's legs heal. He knows all about horses. You have to tell everyone your amazing story."

Gray Feather asked questions all the way back to the Unkpapa camp. Takini did not ride Friendly. He knew his small horse was exhausted. He walked next to Gray Feather as he led Friendly toward the village. The girl carried her bundle of wood, talking nonstop as the two of them reached the edge of the village. In seconds the word spread that the boy named *Survivor* had returned. Gray Feather and Takini were soon surrounded by curious people. Everyone was talking at once. People suddenly became very quiet. Their chief had made his way through the crowd to the two youngsters.

"My people, Takini has returned! Wakan Tanka has guided his feet! Tonight we will hear his story. Now Takini will come with me. He will rest. His faithful horse will be fed and his injuries treated," Sitting Bull proclaimed. "Our warriors have already left to find the two bluecoats who follow our trail."

148

Takini told his story that night. As he stood by the campfire, he was nervous. The more he talked, the easier it became. The people were listening carefully because they realized they were hearing a most amazing story. All were convinced that Wakan Tanka had sent the hawk to help Takini. They were sure Friendly and Lone Dog were given to Takini by the Great Mystery. They knew this boy possessed great powers from Wakan Tanka himself.

As Takini finished his story, Sitting Bull stood to speak. The great chief put his hand on the boy's shoulder and said, "My son, Wakan Tanka has given you special powers. The Great Mystery lives in you. He has given you faithful friends. Friendly and Lone Dog are gifts from Wakan Tanka. The soaring hawk comes from the Great Mystery to lead you and protect you from our enemies. You have been chosen to do great things for our people."

The beloved chief's words rang in Takini's ears. The boy felt lightheaded. All that had happened seemed like a dream. For many years Takini would recall the events he had lived through in the last three days. When Sitting Bull continued to speak, Takini sat at the great man's feet.

"Listen my people," Sitting Bull continued. "Wakan Tanka has sent me a vision. As I slept during the night, a great vision came to me. In it our warriors were fighting a great battle to protect our women and children from hundreds of enemy soldiers. At the end of the fierce fighting, all of the soldiers fell into our camp upside down. My vision is a sign from Wakan Tanka telling me we will soon win a glorious victory against those who come to kill all of our people and rob us of our freedom. We do not look for a fight or to kill anyone. We only wish to live in peace, but if we are attacked we will give our lives to protect our women, children, and elders. Brothers and sisters, enjoy your lives. Enjoy your freedom. We must and we will all stand with each other against any enemy who comes to take our lives or our freedom."

The people sat silently full of wonder, listening to the great chief Sitting Bull's words. Would they really score a great victory against such a powerful enemy? Would Wakan Tanka make their chief's words come true? No one doubted that Sitting Bull possessed amazing spiritual powers. Everyone would hold the chief's words in their hearts. They didn't realize things were already happening that would wash away any doubts about Sitting Bull's vision and the great victory it predicted.

11
A Vision of Death

Six young warriors were sent to find the two soldiers Takini had seen following his people's trail. The young men were told to only find the two soldiers, see what they were doing, and return with a report. They were ordered not to harm the bluecoats and fight only if the soldiers attacked first.

This was 1876 as the bluecoats marked the years. The United States Army had orders to find all Indian people who still roamed free. These people had been given a warning by the United States Government. They were told that as of January 30, 1876, every Indian had to report to a United States Government Agency and never leave. The order stated that Indian people refusing to report to the agency would be considered "hostiles." The United States Army would come with hundreds of well-armed soldiers who would attack and kill all who resisted.

When Takini heard Sitting Bull and the other chiefs talking about these threats from the United States Government, he wondered what was going to happen to him and his people. *Would there be a great war? Would hundreds of soldiers really come to kill Lakota people? Were the two soldiers he had seen coming to find his people? Would they go back and return with hundreds of bluecoats to kill the Lakota? Why were the soldiers so full of hate? Why did they want to rob Indian people of their land and their freedom? Why did they want to kill even women and children and old people? Why couldn't they allow Indian people to be free to find their own happiness?*

The six young warriors returned at noon without finding the two soldiers. The chiefs ordered everyone to pack and prepare to leave. During the following spring months

Takini's people kept moving from place to place. They were always on guard and ready for trouble. As they moved west, the Unkpapa people began to meet more and more Indian people who also searched for lands where they could be free and hunt the buffalo.

When large groups of Indian people met at campfires, all the talk was about the bluecoats and the threats that came from the United States Government. The leaders of the Dakota, the Lakota, the Sans Arcs, the Oglala, the Miniconjoux, the Teton, the Yankton, the Unkpapa, some Northern Cheyenne, and some Blackfeet all planned what they would do if the bluecoats ever came to kill Indian people. Every leader agreed that thousands of warriors would join together and stand up against any attack the bluecoats might make.

In early June a great Sun Dance was held. Never before had a Sun Dance lasted so long and had so many people taken part in it. Sitting Bull was the most inspiring spiritual leader of all. Everyone was amazed by the chief's willingness to suffer great bodily torture during his Sun Dance. Tied to the sturdy center pole with many wooden needles puncturing his flesh, the great chief danced and danced, round and round as his skin was torn from his

153

body. They knew the beloved chief was willing to suffer great pain to inspire all Indian men to commit themselves to their people and be willing to die to protect their women, children, and elders.

Not long after the inspirational dance, Indian scouts returned with news that General Crook's soldiers were camped by Rosebud Creek. Led by the daring Crazy Horse, Indian warriors went to investigate and they were attacked near the soldier's camp. It was a short but fierce battle. Both sides lost many men and many more were wounded. The battle ended suddenly when General Crook and his men retreated to the south. The date of this battle was June 17, 1876.

That night Takini watched as warriors danced for hours celebrating their victory over the invading enemy. He also saw women screaming and crying as they mourned the loss of their men. It was a mixture of sadness and celebration. Some believed this victory was the battle Sitting Bull had seen in his vision, but the great chief told the people they were mistaken. An even bigger battle was coming soon where all the soldiers would die and none would ride away.

Indian leaders were sure the soldiers would be returning with more men and more weapons. The order was given for everyone to pack, load their travois, and begin moving west to the Greasy Grass River. The bluecoats' name for this river was the Little Big Horn. Takini had never seen anything like he was witnessing every day for seven days in a row. Hundreds, even thousands, of Indian people were slowly moving in the same direction. There were women, children, babies, old people, dogs, and thousands of horses. In all Indian history nothing like this had ever happened before. Takini was sure something unbelievable was about to happen.

One week after the Rosebud Creek battle, Takini's people reached the Greasy Grass River. Thousands of Indian people erected their lodges on the west side of the river. The lodges were stretched out for miles. There was plenty of good grass for the large herds of horses. There was good water and lots of firewood for the many cooking fires. That Saturday night, June 24, 1876, Indian people feasted and danced around many fires all along the river far into the early hours of Sunday.

Takini watched it all in complete amazement. Long before the dancing ended, the weary boy fell sound asleep. Takini woke up early that Sunday morning. Most of the exhausted dancers were still sleeping. He found Friendly and took him to the river for a drink. It was a beautiful morning and already very warm. There was no wind. No one had left their beds. Not a thing was stirring near the quiet stream.

As Takini looked out at the beautiful and peaceful land, he felt lucky to be with his own people and the thousands of others gathered at this spectacular place. Friendly finished drinking as Takini continued to look at the gentle slope rising east of the river. At first he could see nothing but grass and sagebrush and a few stunted trees scattered about. Then his eyes caught a movement in the tall sagebrush. He couldn't see what it was, but something seemed to tell him it could mean trouble, and he must go for a closer look. He knew if he went back to his lodge to tell his people whatever he had seen might be gone by the time he returned. He had to take action without delay, or whatever it was could slip away.

Quickly Takini jumped on Friendly, guided him through the shallow river, up the opposite bank, and through the sagebrush toward the spot where he had seen the object move. The boy and his horse moved steadily uphill. Takini's eyes were fixed on the spot where he saw the strange movement. There seemed to be nothing there.

Maybe his eyes had played tricks on him. Maybe he was imagining he saw something. Maybe there was nothing there.

The boy's eyes had not fooled him. He was riding straight for trouble. He was about to become part of a day people all over the world would always remember and talk about. As Friendly and Takini neared the deepest grass on the slope, he was shocked. A man suddenly jumped up and raced down a steep slope into a gully. The boy slid to the ground. He walked to the edge of the ravine in time to see a Crow scout disappear into some dense bushes. In only seconds the Crow man pulled back his bowstring and let an arrow fly toward Takini. The arrow whistled past the boy's ear. He had come only inches from instant death and dropped to the ground before another arrow could be shot.

Takini felt like running. He could easily jump on Friendly and ride to the safety of his village. The boy wondered what he should do next. To retreat would be easy. Takini was confused. Then like a message coming to him from some unknown place, the boy knew he had to keep this enemy in sight. A voice inside his head was telling him he had to find out why this Crow scout had come to spy on his people. If he had any doubts about what to do, his

Crow warrior aims arrow at Takini.

answer came when he looked up. There high above, a majestic hawk glided in great circles on the up drafts of rising air currents.

Takini was sure the hawk was there to guide him. When he saw the hawk gradually move east, he knew the message was from Wakan Tanka. He would head east wherever the hawk led. Takini decided to keep the enemy in sight and follow him wherever he went. Somehow he knew this man was headed to a place where more danger lurked. Takini knew he would have to use all his skills of tracking and staying out of sight. If he was caught, he knew it could mean sudden death.

As the boy squirmed on his stomach to the edge of the ravine, he was just in time to see not one but two Crow scouts mount their horses. He saw their faces for only a split second. Takini was stunned. They were the same two men who had tried to kill him after he had saved the Crow boy's life. Now here they were spying on his people! Takini was more determined than ever to find out what these vicious men were planning next.

The two Crow men rode east away from the Greasy Grass River. Takini could see they were following the gully which led to the top of a ridge. He saw the place where they would come out of the gully and cross the ridge into the next drainage. The boy jumped on Friendly and rode in a wide arc which would keep him out of sight of the enemy scouts. His route would take him to the exact place where the men would leave the gully and start down the other side.

Takini's heart throbbed in his chest. He was leaving the safety of his village. He had no weapon. Lone Dog was still in camp. All he had to help him was his faithful horse and the mighty hawk soaring high above him. As the boy reached the top of the ridge, he kept Friendly in a small clump of scrub pine trees. He was just in time to see the two Crow men emerge from the gully and gallop down the ridge out of view of the Little Big Horn. The Crow scouts had accomplished their mission. They found the Sioux, Northern Cheyenne, and thousands of Indian people camped on the Greasy Grass. They were taking the news to General George Armstrong Custer who with the Seventh Cavalry had been sent to kill the "hostiles." Soon Custer would have all the information needed to map out his plan of attack.

George Armstrong Custer was eager to attack and kill the Indian people. He was thirsty for a great victory over the "hostiles." He knew such a victory would bring him great fame. Custer knew all Americans would hear of his fabulous accomplishments. He would be instantly famous. The American people would surely vote for a conquering hero to be their president just as they voted for General Grant, the great Civil War General. Custer was sure he would have an easy battle and a glorious victory over the hostile savages.

Careful to remain well hidden from view, Takini followed the two scouts. The Crow men were galloping their horses at full speed, looking back now and then to see if they were being followed. The two men were determined to get back to Custer with their report. All the while, Takini rode on and on. The sun was already beating down on the land. The day was oppressively hot and humid. Friendly was soaked with lather as he galloped mile after mile. The boy stopped only once to let Friendly catch his breath and get a quick drink from a small stream. Takini and Friendly were far from the Little Big Horn and safety. The boy did not know he was about to look down on a great army of over 600 bluecoats led by none other than General Custer.

After traveling more than eleven miles, suddenly the two Crow scouts pulled their horses to a stop.

Takini

Immediately Takini sent Friendly down into a gully. The boy jumped to the ground and crawled quickly to the edge of the shallow depression. He was shocked to see the enemy men looking right at his position. *Had they seen him? Should he leap on Friendly and gallop to safety?* Takini just lay there paralyzed with fear. He trembled and could hardly breathe.

Deciding to take one more look, the boy was relieved to see the two Crow men mount up and ride east again. A terrified Takini breathed a sigh of relief. He felt even better when he looked up and spotted his friend, the hawk, gliding above him. The boy did not know the two men had seen him, and had decided to continue on the less than one-mile trip to Custer's camp. They planned to make their report to the General, quickly return to find the boy they had spotted, and make sure Takini would never make it back to his people alive.

More careful than ever, the boy rode Friendly north and out of sight. He finally turned and headed east again. After riding a little more than a half a mile, Takini noticed a sagebrush covered hillside. Knowing this hill would give him a good view of many miles of hills and valleys, the boy rode Friendly slowly toward the slope. As he came to the south side of the hill, Takini's eyes checked the valley below him.

"Whoa! Whoa!" Takini whispered in Friendly's ear.

Instantly the boy hit the ground. What he saw in the distance shocked him. He could not believe his eyes. There were hundreds of bluecoats and their horses. It was the Seventh Cavalry under the command of General George Armstrong Custer. Custer and his men had ridden for thirty-six straight hours in pursuit of the Indian people. The General was eager to win a tremendous and glorious victory. He pushed his men and their horses to near exhaustion. He was afraid the savages would make their escape before he could launch his attack.

At the very moment Takini looked down on this frightening scene, the two scouts were giving Custer their report. They described in great detail exactly where the Indian people were camped on the Little Big Horn. This was all Custer needed to know. Now he could set his plan of attack into motion. He was sure he would be the great conquerer before sunset on this Sunday in June. The last thing the scouts told Custer was that they had been followed by a young boy on a horse. General Custer went into a rage when he heard this news.

Takini

"You idiots! You saw a boy following you, and you did nothing! Are you women? Are you afraid of a boy? If that boy gets back to his people, our chance for a surprise attack will be lost! Get out of here! Find that boy! He has to be stopped! Get moving!"

As the General screamed at the two scouts, one of his captains came up to him. The Captain whispered into Custer's ear. The General turned and looked toward Takini. Custer grabbed a spyglass from the Captain and held it to his eye. Only Takini's head was above the sagebrush. He thought he couldn't be seen. He didn't know what a spyglass could do. There the bluecoat general stood, looking right at Takini. Custer could even see Friendly's head behind and above the boy.

Custer turned and shouted at the Crow scouts, "The boy is up there looking down at my army. Move! Get him! When you catch him, silence him forever! Go!"

Not knowing what was happening below him, Takini slowly moved away. He led Friendly from the hillside. The boy realized every second counted now and not one could be wasted. Sitting Bull, Crazy Horse, and all the warriors must know about this huge army which was only twelve miles from the Indian camp. Takini knew he could not allow his people to be surprised by almost seven hundred, heavily armed, mounted bluecoats.

"Go Friendly! It's up to you and me! We have to warn our people! Many could be killed! We can't let it happen! Go Friendly! Run like you have never run before! You can do it!"

Friendly was already dripping with lather in the oppressive heat and humidity. Takini felt nothing at all. He was numb with fear. He could think about only one thing: making it back to his people in time. The boy didn't care what happened to him as long as he warned his people before it was too late. He was ready to die if he had to.

Takini didn't realize the Crow warriors were already closing in on him. How would a helpless unarmed boy ever outsmart and escape two well-armed warriors? If this Lakota boy ever needed Wakan Tanka, it was now! The Great Mystery would have to be his guardian and protect him. The clock was ticking on this historic day, a day the world would always remember.

12
No Turning Back

Friendly was moving as fast as he safely could on the steep hillside. It was very difficult for the small horse to keep his footing and avoid slipping and sliding downward. When they finally reached the valley floor, Friendly broke into a full gallop. Takini kept looking back and off to each side to see if he was being followed. Friendly was galloping fast enough to create a slight breeze which gave the boy welcome relief from the torrid heat and humidity.

Takini

Having looked back many times and seeing nothing, Takini felt quite sure he was not being followed. He began to relax a little. Then something seemed to tell the boy to look south. One glance filled his entire body with terror. Only a half a mile away, there they were. The same two Crow scouts were galloping at full speed at an angle to cut off Friendly and Takini from any chance of escape.

"Friendly! Here they come! Go, Friendly! Run! You can do it!"

The Crow scouts had huge powerful horses. They were rapidly gaining on Friendly. Takini realized there was no chance of out-running the two enemy warriors. Hope was fading. The boy had visions of hundreds of bluecoats attacking and killing his people. All hope of making it back in time to warn them seemed lost. Takini was preparing himself to die. He knew he had made his best effort to save his people. If he had to die, he was ready. Maybe Wakan Tanka was letting him give his life for his people. The boy looked to the heavens and asked the Great Mystery to deliver him from the two charging warriors. He prayed that Wakan Tanka would let him reach the Greasy Grass River before it was too late.

The Crow men were only a quarter of a mile away when Takini heard a shrill, screeching sound. The boy looked over his shoulder and saw a glorious sight! The great hawk came swooping down toward him. The majestic bird passed only ten feet above Takini's head. The boy smiled and waved. The hawk dipped its wings three times.

"Go, Friendly! Hawk is here to save us! Follow the hawk! He is Wakan Tanka's messenger!"

Suddenly the hawk made a sharp turn to the north. The bird was heading toward a side canyon at full speed. Friendly followed the swift flying bird as it zigzagged only ten feet off the ground. Takini stretched to see into the canyon. It didn't look good! Something was seriously wrong! This was a blind canyon with steep walls on all three sides! The boy could see no way out! *Was the hawk leading him the wrong way? How could this be a way to escape the two killers?* It seemed like the hawk was leading the boy into a death trap, but it was too late to turn back! Takini had to ride on into the canyon and hope for the best.

At the mouth of the canyon, Friendly galloped through a buffalo wallow, a sandy bowl where buffalo loved to roll over and over in the sand to get relief from fleas and other insects. This wallow had been used by buffalo for hundreds of years and the fine grainy sand was several feet deep, much like an ocean beach. The sand had come from deposits of sandstone eroded by melting snow and rain storms. As Friendly and Takini passed the buffalo wallow, the boy heard a blood- curdling cry. The two warriors were closing in, and Takini knew they had him trapped once and for all. Soon they would kill him and be able to return to General Custer and report their mission had been accomplished. They would have Takini silenced forever.

Takini was running out of space. Wakan Tanka's hawk would have to create a miracle soon, or the boy would face a horrible death. The enemy was already reaching the buffalo wallow. They were less than a hundred yards from Takini. At the instant the two warriors rode into the sandy wallow, a microburst of wind came out of nowhere and hit the canyon. The violent wind created a funnel of whirling sand. It was like a miniature tornado. Fine grains of sand filled the warriors' eyes. Their startled horses reared up on their hind legs, tossing their riders into the sand. The terrified horses galloped away leaving their riders flat on their backs in the sand.

Takini looked back just in time to witness this miracle. He saw the men jump to their feet and begin rubbing the sand from their eyes. The boy thought about turning around and riding past the two warriors and out of the

Crow warriors and horses get caught in a sudden sand-
storm as Takini heads into a blind canyon.

canyon. In a split second he forgot about that idea. The enemy warriors were still a threat. It would take only one well-aimed arrow to end Takini's life. All the boy could do was ride on and hope for another miracle.

This canyon was not very long. Takini could see it ended at a steep wall of rock blocking any chance of escape. There seemed to be no way out. The boy was losing hope when suddenly the hawk began flapping its wings wildly. The bird was sitting on a sharp rock protruding from the canyon wall.

Takini was almost to the wall when the hawk took flight. The hawk glided toward the canyon floor as if it planned to land on the ground. As the boy's eyes followed the hawk's flight, he noticed a bright white object lying on the ground at the base of the canyon wall. *Was it a white rock? What made it so bright?* The answers came when the hawk reached the white object. Instantly the white thing moved. It rose up on four legs. Takini could not believe his eyes. There right in front of him stood a buffalo, a spectacular white buffalo. An albino buffalo was one in a million. It was the most beautiful animal Takini had ever seen. He almost forgot he was still in great danger and needed to find a way to escape this trap.

The stunning white buffalo seemed to stare directly at Friendly and Takini. Suddenly the spectacular creature trotted off to the right and disappeared completely. The boy urged Friendly on toward the spot where the white buffalo had disappeared from view. Takini was sure the hawk had led him to the white buffalo, and Wakan Tanka had placed the beautiful animal there to save him.

When Takini came to the canyon wall and looked to the right, there was the buffalo again. The white buffalo was moving up a thin strip of sand in a narrow gully leading up and out of the canyon. Takini was positive Wakan Tanka had led him to this escape route. The hawk was again the messenger sent to guide the boy to the white buffalo. Takini realized Wakan Tanka had sent the wind to churn up sand and stop the warriors in their tracks. The boy looked to the heavens and whispered his prayer of thanksgiving to Wakan Tanka. At the top of the drainage there stood the fabulous white buffalo with the hawk circling only twenty feet above the animal. Going up the drainage toward freedom, Takini remembered his mother's words.

Minutes before his mother's death she said, "My son, talk often with the Great Mystery. He will be with you to guide you."

Takini

"Mother, I remember your words. I will always obey. I will talk often to the Great Mystery. Wakan Tanka is with me today. He will help me warn my people in time."

As Takini rode Friendly up the narrow gully and out of the canyon, the white buffalo and the hawk disappeared. Looking back into the canyon the boy could see the two enemy warriors still rubbing their eyes. Without their horses these killers would have no way of stopping Takini. The two men had no idea what happened to the boy they were pursuing. By the time their eyes cleared, he would be far from this canyon. Takini was startled to see how exhausted Friendly looked. His faithful horse was soaking wet with sweat. The boy slowly slid off his weary horse.

"Good boy, Friendly! You saved my life again! Wakan Tanka is with us! The Great Mystery sent the hawk and the white buffalo to save us from the enemy! We can rest for a few minutes! Then you must take me to our people! We can save many lives! You can do it, I know you can!" Takini whispered as he stroked Friendly's neck.

From his position high above the valley the boy could see for miles. He carefully examined a valley to his right and to the north. Takini was excited to see signs of a trail made by hundreds of other Indian people. He was sure this track was made by a band of Indian people who were headed to the Little Big Horn camp. The boy would wait only a few more minutes, and then head down to this trail. In this valley he would be out of sight of the bluecoats and General Custer and would be able to travel fast as possible.

Before getting on Friendly to head west again, Takini took one more look at the two enemy scouts. The two men were headed out of the canyon on foot to find their missing horses. The two horses were nowhere in sight. The boy was happy to see the two enemy men helplessly wandering away on foot.

As Takini turned to mount Friendly, he noticed something moving at the east end of the valley. That was the exact spot the two Crow scouts had come from after leaving General Custer and the Seventh Cavalry. The boy's eyes were glued to the movement. He was soon shocked to see a column of bluecoats riding two-by-two in a long continuous line. In front of the column two riders emerged, one bearing an American flag and the other the flag of the Seventh Cavalry.

Takini watched the flag bearers lead the soldiers south toward a gentle sloping hill. *Why were they going south? Didn't they know the way to the Little Big Horn? Didn't the*

Takini

Crow scouts tell them where the Indian people were camped?
The boy realized he had to stay long enough to learn what
the bluecoats were doing, and where they were going.
Almost two hundred bluecoats had emerged from the trees
when suddenly two more flag bearers appeared. These two
riders were leading a second column of soldiers heading
southwest.

Takini was stunned to see what was unfolding before his
eyes. He was sure he was looking at the beginning of the
march to the Greasy Grass and the attack on his people.
The boy was fascinated by the scary scene. He had never
seen anything like this before. Takini knew he was gaining
important information he could take back to Crazy Horse
and the other war leaders. Time was critical now, but the
boy understood the importance of waiting just a little
longer so he could discover exactly what the bluecoats
were doing. This information could save many Indian
lives and maybe help his people win a great victory over
the invaders.

Takini's wait paid off. A third column of bluecoats came
into view headed by two flag bearers. These soldiers headed
straight west on the same course Takini had taken to reach
the place where he had discovered General Custer and his

Seventh Cavalry. The boy understood the army's plan. They would attack in three groups in the attempt to cut off any chance of escape by the surprised Indian people. Takini had seen enough. Not another second could be wasted. He had to outrun the enemy and make it back to his people and give them the vital information needed to survive the attack by General Custer and the Seventh Cavalry.

"Let's go, Friendly! You can do it! You can beat the blue-coat horses! Friendly, we have to make it! We can save our people! Go, Friendly, Go!"

Takini rode Friendly into the northern valley out of sight of the bluecoats. Soon they were galloping along the well-worn trail. The heat and humidity were oppressive. Friendly was gasping for every breath. It seemed like the small horse knew his master needed him to keep going no matter what happened. The trail was hot and dusty and appeared to be endless when actually the distance to the Little Big Horn was just a little more than ten miles.

After nine miles of galloping at full speed, Friendly started slowing as he climbed a gentle slope. At the top of the ridge, Takini's faithful horse stumbled twice. The second time Friendly nearly fell to the ground. The small horse was suffering from heat exhaustion and dehydration.

Takini

Friendly was nearing the end of his ability to go on. The courageous horse had given everything he had to carry his master back with the news of the impending attack. Just as Takini looked down on the valley where his people were camped, Friendly collapsed forward on his front knees. The boy jumped to the ground.

"Friendly, you did it! We made it in time! You are the greatest horse ever! Come, we can walk down to our people! You can rest! You can take a long drink of cool water!"

Suddenly Takini heard a dog barking wildly. Lone Dog came charging up the hill at full speed. The dog jumped into Takini's arms. The boy dropped to his knees hugging his excited dog.

"Lone Dog, I'm back! We have to run to our camp! Friendly is weary! He will follow us! Let's go!"

Being careful not to stumble and fall, Takini sprinted down the slope as fast as he could go. Lone Dog raced on ahead. Friendly followed at a slow but steady pace. As the boy neared the river, he heard Indian boys and girls splashing in the water of the Little Big Horn River. They were having a great time and were escaping the torrid heat. Gray Feather was the first one to stop swimming and look up and spot Lone Dog, Takini, and Friendly coming toward the river.

Takini was still a half a mile away when Gray Feather saw him and his animal friends coming. She saw Takini running downhill waving his arms. The girl watched him take a bad fall, jump up, and run some more. Gray Feather ran to her lodge to tell her father what she had seen. Gray Feather's father ran to his horse, mounted up, and rode out to investigate. Soon the man was pulling Takini up so they could ride double back to the village. As fast as he could talk, Takini was telling Gray Feather's father the whole story. The man immediately kicked his horse into a full gallop.

As soon as Gray Feather's father crossed the river, he pulled his horse to an abrupt stop. The man jumped to the ground and pulled Takini down next to him. The man ran to Crazy Horse. The great war leader came running to hear the boy's report. Crazy Horse listened to Takini's every word. Crazy Horse had many questions. Takini answered every question with exact details. After finishing with his questions, Crazy Horse spoke some amazing words.

"Takini, you are a good and brave boy! Wakan Tanka has guided you! He has chosen you to help save our people! You are blessed with powerful medicine! Now I must go! Now our warriors will prepare to fight!"

Takini

Crazy Horse said some of the same words Takini's dying mother had said. Takini was sure his mother's wishes were coming true. The boy and Gray Feather returned to the river. There on the east side of the river Friendly stood in the water drinking his fill. Takini jumped into the river and waded over to Friendly. The boy splashed water onto his horse's back and neck. Gray Feather watched Takini lead his weary horse through the water toward her. The boy was deep in thought. He could still see the three columns of bluecoats riding two-by-two on their way to kill his people. Every detail of that morning would live with Takini the rest of his life.

As Takini and Gray Feather stood next to Friendly rubbing the gallant horse's body, word was spreading through the village about the approaching enemy. There would be just enough time to get the message to all the people spread out for miles along the river. The sun was high overhead and the day was half over when the first bluecoats came into view on the eastern ridges above the Little Big Horn River. Takini, Gray Feather, all the children, the women, and the old people were led west away from the Greasy Grass and the approaching Seventh Cavalry. The women and children would hear the rifles, the war cries,

180

and the sounds of dying men. Not even one bluecoat would make it through to the women and children. Takini kept Friendly and Lone Dog close to him as he helped other boys herd the spare horses west.

The great battle would rage on in the torrid heat of that Sunday afternoon, June 25, 1876. Thanks to a young boy called *Survivor*, a hawk, a white buffalo, and a faithful horse, the Sioux, the Northern Cheyenne, and other tribal warriors would be ready to defend their women, children, and old people. Chief Sitting Bull's vision of a great Indian victory was about to come true. That afternoon General Custer's hundreds of bluecoats would fall into the Indian camp upside down. Soon news of the Battle of the Little Big Horn would spread east and capture the imagination of millions of people worldwide.

Epilogue

Students of the Little Big Horn Battle believe General Custer made some fatal errors in his haste to engage the "hostiles." First, Custer marched his men for thirty-six straight hours with hardly any rest and the men were far ahead of their supply wagons. Second, Custer was sure the Indian warriors would turn and run from the superior force of his Seventh Cavalry. The third fatal mistake was Custer's decision to divide his forces into three separate columns. Captain Benteen took a third of the men south to make sure any retreating Indians would be caught. Major Reno took a third of the men west to hit the middle of the Indian village. Custer took over 200 men to attack the north end of the large village. By fighting with exhausted men and horses far ahead of their supplies, underestimating the number and determination of the

Indian people, and splitting his troops into three groups, Custer doomed the Seventh Cavalry to a terrible defeat.

After the Battle of the Little Big Horn, the many bands of Indian people scattered throughout the West. Sitting Bull and his Unkpapa people kept moving and avoided further trouble. The winter of 1876-77 was especially harsh and Sitting Bull's people suffered greatly.

In May of 1877, Sitting Bull led his people to safety in Canada. After four years in Canada, Sitting Bull returned to the United States with his people. But the days of free-roaming Indians were ending. Sitting Bull joined Buffalo Bill Cody's Wild West Show. On a cold December morning in 1890, Sitting Bull was murdered.

Children like Takini and Gray Feather adjusted to a new way of life after the Battle of Little Big Horn. No longer were they free to live in teepees on the open plains. First they lived near a United States Government Agency and then they moved to a reservation set aside for their people. Today Lakota people are working hard to preserve their language and cultural traditions. Most Lakota people are now living on reservations in South Dakota.

Since that difficult time in the nineteenth century, Indian people have come forward to serve gallantly in every war the United States has had to fight to maintain our freedom and our way of life. Now many young Indian people are dedicating their lives to the improvement of their tribes. A wonderful Lakota College offers them excellent education and training. The college helps keep cultural traditions alive and works to develop the skills young Indian people need to compete in a modern world and to be the new leaders of a proud people.

Ken Thomasma

Ken Thomasma, a seasoned teacher, principal, and media specialist, now spends his time as a writing workshop leader and professional storyteller. He is concerned that children have accurate information about Americans who lived in the West before white settlers came. A careful researcher as well as a gifted storyteller, Ken checks out details and descriptions with tribal leaders to make sure that his material is not only historically accurate but also welcomed and appreciated by Indians themselves.

There are now nine books in the popular **Amazing Indian Children** series. Three of the books have won the Wyoming Children's Book Award: *Naya Nuki, Pathki Nana,* and *Moho Wat.* The books have also been nominated for the Colorado Children's Book Award and the Colorado Blue Spruce Award. *Naya Nuki* was nominated for the Utah Children's Book Award. The books have been translated into Japanese, Danish, Dutch, Norwegian, and Eskimo dialects for Greenland. Currently a movie is being made of the *Naya Nuki* story.

Ken, his wife, Bobbi, and the younger Thomasmas—Dan, Cathy, grandson Oliver, and granddaughter Melissa—enjoy spectacular views of ever-changing scenery from their homes located on the south border of Grand Teton National Park in Jackson, Wyoming.

Agnes Vincen Talbot

Agnes Vincen Talbot's love of the native American West began in her childhood days growing up in Boise, Idaho. After developing her significant natural talent, she moved to Connecticut, continued her art studies for fourteen years, and then returned to Boise. She is a disciplined art historian who insists on authenticity and demanding detail in her sculpture and paintings. Her intricate illustrations in this book reflect her love for the rich history of the American West. This is the third book she has illustrated. She sculpted a beautiful bronze of Sacajawea and her baby for the Fort Lemhi Indian Community. A photo of her bronze is featured on the U.S. Mint Web page in connection with the Sacajawea dollar coin.

AMAZING INDIAN CHILDREN SERIES

Naya Nuki: Shoshoni Girl Who Ran
An eleven-year-old plans a daring escape from an enemy village and makes a hazardous wilderness trek back to her homeland.

Soun Tetoken: Nez Perce Boy Tames a Stallion
A mute youngster survives the tragic Nez Perce War and remains true to his uncle, Chief Joseph.

Om-kas-toe: Blackfeet Twin Captures an Elkdog
Twins play a role in bringing the first horse to the Blackfeet people.

Kunu: Winnebago Boy Escapes
A captured boy and his grandfather secretly make a dugout canoe and escape down the treacherous Missouri River.

Pathki Nana: Kootenai Girl Solves a Mystery
A girl who believes she is a failure uses all her resources to escape an evil man who wants to end her life.

Moho Wat: Sheepeater Boy Attempts a Rescue
A one-handed boy sets out to rescue the beautiful Wind Flower who has been kidnapped by enemy warriors.

Amee-nah: Zuni Boy Runs the Race of His Life
Boy heroically overcomes ridicule and major foot surgery to run the race of his life.

Doe Sia: Bannock Girl and the Handcart Pioneers
Ten-year-old girls, Doe Sia and Emma, lost in the early fierce blizzard of 1856, stuggle to survive and find their way back to their people

Takini: Lakota Boy Alerts Sitting Bull
A young boy, along with his faithful horse and beloved dog, plays a major part in events leading up to the Battle of the Little Big Horn.

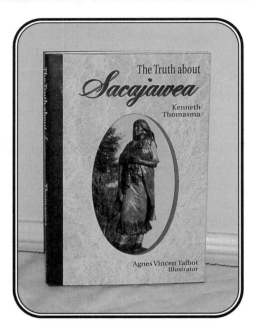

The Truth about Sacajawea

A reliable, carefully documented, picture of the twenty-one months the resourceful teenager Sacajawea spent with the Lewis and Clark Corps of Discovery.